"Can we sit down and hold a civilized argument?" Kash asked as he glanced around. "I never conduct important discussions in boudoirs smelling of cinnamon bath soap. Do you think of yourself as a cinnamon bun, a cookie, or a steaming cup of hot spiced cider?"

Rebecca stiffened and gave him a fierce look. "A cold vanilla milkshake with poison in it. Please, take a big sip."

"Invitations were made to be accepted."

He pulled her to him and kissed her lightly. Her sharp gasp broke against his mouth. He held her in a loose embrace, one she could easily pull away from, but instead of shoving him away, she twisted her mouth tightly on his. Kash was astonished at his impulse and her reaction, but he refused to break the kiss.

He felt her tremble against him. Slowly her hand dropped to his shoulder and clenched his soft cotton undershirt. Her mouth was as mobile as his own, and just as aggressive. Waves of desire shot through him, stunning him. He was far from being a stranger to desire, but not this scalding, elemental sense of losing himself in her.

Dragging her hands over his shoulders, Rebecca kneaded the hard muscles and felt them flex in response. He was the shadowy force she'd been drawn to all her life, the visitor in her nighttime dreams, the first man who'd ever caused her to forget everything but the primitive need for fulfillment.

WHAT ARE *LOVESWEPT* ROMANCES?

They are stories of true romance and touching emotion. We believe those two very important ingredients are constants in our highly sensual and very believable stories in the *LOVESWEPT* line. Our goal is to give you, the reader, stories of consistently high quality that may sometimes make you laugh, sometimes make you cry, but are always fresh and creative and contain many delightful surprises within their pages.

Most romance fans read an enormous number of books. Those they truly love, they keep. Others may be traded with friends and soon forgotten. We hope that each *LOVESWEPT* romance will be a treasure—a "keeper." We will always try to publish

LOVE STORIES YOU'LL NEVER FORGET
BY AUTHORS YOU'LL ALWAYS REMEMBER

The Editors

Loveswept 503

Deborah Smith
Heart of the Dragon

BANTAM BOOKS
NEW YORK · TORONTO · LONDON · SYDNEY · AUCKLAND

HEART OF THE DRAGON
A Bantam Book / October 1991

*LOVESWEPT® and the wave device are registered
trademarks of Bantam Books, a division of
Bantam Doubleday Dell Publishing Group, Inc.
Registered in U.S. Patent
and Trademark Office and elsewhere.*

*If you would be interested in receiving protective vinyl
covers for your Loveswept books, please write to this address
for information:*

> Loveswept
> Bantam Books
> P.O. Box 985
> Hicksville, NY 11802

ISBN 0-553-44112-4

Published simultaneously in the United States and Canada

*Bantam Books are published by Bantam Books, a division
of Bantam Doubleday Dell Publishing Group, Inc. Its trademark, consisting of the words "Bantam Books" and the
portrayal of a rooster, is Registered in U.S. Patent and
Trademark Office and in other countries. Marca Registrada.
Bantam Books, 666 Fifth Avenue, New York, New York
10103.*

Heart of the Dragon

One

Though he stood in cool, elegant silence at the window, Kashadlin Santelli's insides churned with impatience as he awaited the arrival of a woman he'd never met. His stillness came from lifelong practice, from an emotional distance he cultivated as a shield. But questions boiled inside him, and he leaned closer to the large, ebony-rimmed window two stories above the street.

Kash stroked the pale silk curtain, thinking distract-edly that it was as smooth and soft as a woman's skin, and as cool as Rebecca Brown's nerves must be. The combination intrigued him. She must have extraordi-nary self-confidence if she was here in Bangkok for the reason he suspected. The Nalinat family was inventive, to have gone all the way to America to hire a spy.

Yes, Rebecca Brown was a puzzle. He would meet her, assess her intentions, and judge her honesty for him-self.

With a slight smile he silently warned her that his own nerves were far more than a match for hers. He was skilled at uncovering treachery and protecting others from it. If Rebecca Brown had been hired to cause trouble for his client, he would open her as easily as a lotus flower and pluck her secrets out. Innocence of any kind was an elusive treasure in life. He had learned that even as a child. Especially as a child.

Shaking off a dark memory, he glanced around the office he'd arranged to have for the afternoon, and prided himself on his judgment. For atmosphere he'd chosen a building with traditional decor, where gold dragons scowled from carved teak wall panels and the finest Thai silk covered heavily embroidered pillows piled on a long red sofa. The room's desk had majestic tiger heads sculpted into each corner of the mahogany top, and on the top lay a pad of pale parchment paper, a slender gold pen, and for decoration a smooth block of jade as big as a brick—hard, unyielding, its purpose a mystery. He wanted her to worry about the mysteries, to consider that she was tampering with a people and a place where the rules were ancient and not at all like her own.

And him—she was tampering with him. He wanted her to realize that he was unlike any man she'd known before. If she was involved in the scheme he suspected, he wanted her to be afraid of him.

The street below him teemed with small golden-skinned people in a mixture of Western and Asian dress. Saffron-robed Buddhist monks walked among businessmen wearing suits and ties. Cars and buses jostled with bicycles and puttering open-air *tuk tuks*, motorized three-wheel scooters with passenger compartments in the back.

Vendors in colorful shirts and trousers and broad-brimmed straw hats squatted among their wares on the sidewalks outside modern boutiques filled with Western goods. Kash knew that everything, from a hot meal to a fine diamond, from the commonplace and legal to the exotic and *very* illegal, could be purchased on a Bangkok street.

Physically he didn't fit in with the people below. He was much too tall and broad-shouldered, barbaric by their standards. And his facial features only hinted at his Asian heritage. But inside, a part of him would always be the tough, streetwise little boy who belonged to this part of the world.

Through the curtain he glimpsed the white sedan as it pulled up at the curb below. His heart rate quickened from the anticipation of meeting Rebecca Brown and hearing for himself the ludicrous story she'd been telling all over the city. When the driver opened a rear door, Kash turned away, preferring to wait until she was in his office, face to face, before he saw her the first time. The curtain's silk made a sensual whisper as he drew heavy drapes over it.

Rebecca Brown slid a hand under her hair and delicately adjusted the hearing aid in her right ear. Her Thai escort, the slender, unhappy-looking man who'd hardly spoken a word in the long ride from her hotel, was now trying to tell her something. But they were in the middle of a bustling sidewalk, and several Thai businessmen were gesturing politely for her to move her somewhat tall, awkward self out of their paths. She remembered a scene outside her hotel yesterday. An elephant had wandered away from his owner and into the street, blocking every vehicle larger than a motor scooter.

Now she knew how the elephant felt.

She nodded to the businessman apologetically and pressed her palms together in a prayerful gesture beneath her chin. The Thais called it a *wai*. It could mean hello, good-bye, or in this case, pardon me, I'm goofy, she thought with embarrassment. The men detoured around her gracefully, with strained smiles.

"Pardon me, what did you say?" she asked her escort again, craning her head down to his and touching the sleeve of his white suit.

His eyebrows shot up. She pulled her hand away and winced inwardly. She kept forgetting that it wasn't proper for women to touch men in public, even when the man was a boyfriend or husband, or in this case, a scowling executive from the Vatan Silk Company who'd been given the obviously unpleasant task of taking her—finally!—to meet Mayura Vatan.

"You will go upstairs alone," her escort said, louder this time. "I leave you now."

"But—"

"Office number two-two, on the second floor." He made a curt *wai* to her and turned toward the car.

Rebecca resisted an urge to tug at his sleeve. "Is Ms. Vatan expecting me? What building is this? Does the company have offices here too? I thought we were going to the other offices, the ones I've visited before."

"You will see." The driver opened the door so that her escort could slide into the sedan's dark interior. In the noonday heat the car's air-conditioning burst toward Rebecca like a wonderful cool fog. "Are you going to wait here?" she asked hurriedly, brushing away the feathery hair stuck to her damp forehead.

"No, but you can always find a taxi. Good day, Ms. Brown."

A little flustered, Rebecca stared after the car until it merged with the bumper-to-bumper traffic. Well, rudeness and desertion wouldn't stop a real adventurer, she told herself, and retucked her damp white blouse into a long, matching skirt. Toting her soft leather satchel and feeling a little foolish, she went inside the office building and found an elevator. The building's tenants were listed on a small chart encased in glass on the dark enameled wall adjacent to the elevator. She saw office 2-2, but found no name beside it.

A knot of dread and bewilderment grew in her stomach on the short ride up. The door opened into the small lobby of a single suite. She stepped out slowly, studying the heavy double doors facing the elevator. They had ornate brass handles in the form of curving snakes and were inset with glistening lacquered red panels. The effect was exotic and forbidding. Her heart began pounding as if the doors hid a hungry tiger. There were still tigers in the mountains of northern Thailand, she recalled.

Rebecca smiled tightly. She hadn't come all the way from Iowa to be scared off by her own imagination, vivid and colorful though it was.

She went to the doors and knocked firmly. The sudden loud thudding of footsteps on the other side made her eardrum ache, and she winced. She'd forgotten to turn the hearing aid down to normal. Throwing a hand up to her ear, she nervously fiddled with the volume.

As the footsteps halted and the doors clicked open, she scooted the control in the wrong direction. A high-pitched electronic squeal zapped her ear.

When the doors swung back, the first thing she saw, through the eye that wasn't squinted shut in pain, was a masculine vision that conjured up jumbled thoughts of pale champagne, hard, cool onyx, and satin. And the first thing the tall, darkly glorious male vision saw was her grabbing her right ear frantically, while her purse fell off her left shoulder and slid past the scuffed brown satchel hanging from her left hand, then fell by her left foot, where, in her haste to grab the purse, she lost her balance and stepped on it.

Rebecca was too stunned by the man standing in the doorway to be deeply embarrassed; her clownish lack of grace was a dearly prized part of who she was, as essential as her sense of humor. It kept her world a little off-center, and made her career as a cartoonist successful. She simply drew the world the way she lived.

Besides, this man made embarrassment the least of her worries. More important was the lightning snap of feminine alertness, the feeling that her blood and breath were frozen in expectation, and that she couldn't take her eyes off him.

Kash was having the same difficulty with her. He'd expected someone clever enough to make herself seem likable and ordinary, not eccentric. Rebecca Brown peered up at him from under feathery brunette bangs, while one hand clutched oddly at her right ear and the other wrestled a white purse from under her white sandal. But if her actions were strange, her neat white blouse and long cotton skirt were the height of unremarkable tourist attire.

Then she flashed him a cheerful, if tentative, grin that turned her face into a merry invitation to smile back, and she straightened, apparently not embarrassed by whatever the hell it was she had been doing or its results. She was slender, but her figure was not the least bit boyish. He realized that he was giving her the kind of slow, head-to-toe assessment that he never gave a woman, because it lacked subtlety and respect. He didn't hesitate to admire a woman who wanted to be looked at, but neither did he stare the way he was staring at Rebecca Brown right then.

Rebecca managed to keep smiling even when the object of her friendliness lost his surprised, somewhat benign expression and looked her up and down as if calculating whether he *wanted* to undress her with his eyes. That look—as much as she resented it—had a hypnotic effect, making her knees weak and her muscles feel heavy.

She'd never gotten many outright sexual stares back in Iowa, or felt her own heart thumping because of them. She'd never run across a man who seemed to be caught between cultures, either, one with slightly tilted eyes, a strong, sculptured nose, a hint of gold in his skin, and hair the soft black color of charred wood. Where did he belong? Where was he from? And—good lord, she'd almost forgotten what she was there for— what was he doing there in place of Mayura Vatan?

"I'm at a loss," she said finally, as she hooked her purse back over her shoulder and casually pulled her hair over the hearing aid to hide it. "I think you know who I am, but I don't know who you are. I came here to see Mayura Vatan."

"I'm her representative," he answered, his words measured. "She asked me to hear your story and report the details to her."

His voice was low and compelling, a cognac that slid warmly through her veins, and Rebecca was surprised to hear not only an American accent but a slightly southern one. It gave his voice an elegant lilt. She scrutinized him with her head tilted to the left side, to catch each nuance of tone with her good ear.

Kash cursed her strange response silently. It was exasperating and put him on the defensive. Perhaps she'd planned it that way. He stepped back and swept an arm toward the room. "Please, come into my office. My name is Santelli. Kashadlin Santelli, Ms. Brown."

"Do you work for Vatan Silk? I think I've met every executive in the company during the past two weeks."

"I doubt it," he said with a hint of amusement that could have warmed her, except it didn't reach his dark, shrewd eyes. "It's far too large a company. You could have gone on meeting unimportant executives for a long time before you accomplished your goal. But you're lucky—they've sent you straight to me. We'll settle this quickly."

She stiffened and drew her shoulders back. "I was told that Mayura Vatan would be here. I've spent so much time trying to see her, and when I got a phone call from her office today, I thought she'd be waiting. Are you telling me she's not here?"

"Yes. I'm sorry you were lied to. But please, come inside, where we can discuss this further."

"At least you're blunt about what's going on."

"You and I haven't determined 'what's going on' yet." He gestured again toward an office of sparse but luxurious furnishings. He seemed to be pointing straight at a thick red sofa strewn with beautiful pillows. "Let's discuss your claim," he said softly.

Rebecca wasn't certain she wanted to sink into a wickedly plush sofa with this man. His unusual name, Kashadlin Santelli, kept revolving in her mind and distracting her. He was at least six inches taller than she, and that added to his aura of command. She bristled at the way he made requests sound like orders.

"You have nothing to worry about, Ms. Brown," he said smoothly. "I'm a trustworthy employee of Mayura Vatan."

Rebecca walked into the big, dark office with a pleasant smile stamped on her mouth. Richly embroidered drapes covered the windows. The only light came from an ornate brass lamp on an enameled black table in the room's center. Her stomach twisted with apprehension, but also anticipation. Good Lord, the man was playing some kind of mind game with her. She stopped in the middle of the room and stood rigidly. She hoped she looked resolute. "The only thing that worries me is whether I'll have to see a dozen more people like you before I'm allowed to meet Ms. Vatan."

"No, as I've already said, you've reached the top this time." He shut the doors behind her. She refused to glance back over her shoulder to watch him, but every hair on her neck stood on end. She pictured the imaginary tiger prowling up to her and— Stop it, she ordered herself silently.

When he cupped her elbow, she felt the heat of his palm radiate through her whole body. And he was suddenly so close that she smelled the faint, clovelike scent of his cologne, along with the more subtle scents of fine cloth and freshly showered masculine skin. She tried to breathe steadily but couldn't subdue a mental image of the lean golden body under his exquisitely cut suit. He wasn't brawny-looking, but his shoulders were broad and conveyed powerful grace. The hand that closed lightly on her elbow had a wide, hard palm, and long, confident fingers. She glanced back, dry-mouthed.

His expression was aloof. If there had been a hint of

warmth in it before, it was now as neutral as the crisp lines of his suit. A black suit, a pale gray shirt, and a black tie with only the finest of silver stripes, Rebecca noted. Thoroughly Western, and solemn.

"May I get you a drink?" he asked.

"No, thank you. I just want to know why I'm getting shuffled around every time I ask to see Ms. Vatan. Who are you exactly?"

"Sit down, please." He guided her to the decadent-looking sofa. At the risk of appearing nervous, she glanced around for a less disturbing place to sit, but there was only the upholstered office chair behind his desk. Rebecca's pride rebelled. She might not be his equal in this game—whatever it was—but she wasn't going to run for safety.

She reconsidered that choice when he was seated beside her on the sofa. He lounged back, sinking into the shimmering silk pillows with arms propped on them as if he were on a throne. Rebecca found her knee against his. Moving it would admit that she felt uncomfortable. She sat back in her corner of the sofa and crossed her legs away from him. Now her other knee was against his. She gave up.

"I want to see Ms. Vatan," she said flatly, laying her satchel on her lap and unbuttoning the latch. "Are you her assistant?"

"No, I'm her bodyguard."

Rebecca stared at him. "Bodyguard?"

"Security coordinator, if you prefer," he amended. "I perform a variety of services." He smiled, and she caught a flash of predatory white teeth. Mayura Vatan's lover, I bet, she thought instantly. An electric snap of curiosity and envy shot through her.

His lips were full, his mouth wide. It could have been a fantastically sensual mouth—and must be, when he was doing something with a woman besides trying to intimidate her—but right then it had a sarcastic tilt at one corner. He lifted a hand slightly, addressing her.

"Are you a dangerous woman, Ms. Brown? Does my client need protection from you?"

Rebecca thought he was teasing. There was just enough humor in his tone to make it possible. But also enough warning to bring her anger to full bloom. She clenched her satchel with both hands and spoke between gritted teeth. "I've said this about a dozen times. Now I'll tell *you*. Maybe someday, someone will believe me. *I'm not here to cause trouble.*"

"You realize, surely, that a claim such as yours, against a young woman of wealth and prestige—"

"I'm not making a claim *against* anyone. I'm trying to make someone believe the truth. I just want to meet Mayura Vatan."

"Because?" he asked, and let the word hang expectantly, as if he hadn't already been briefed on the whole story.

"Because she and I are half sisters!"

Kashadlin Santelli's eyes narrowed. It appeared that hearing this outrageous-sounding statement from her own lips only confirmed his opinion of her—and that opinion wasn't good, she could tell. "I'm fascinated," he said dryly. "Please go on."

"What's the point? You're only the latest in a long line of Vatan family employees who'll smile politely and never believe a word I say."

"No. You see, I'm the one who determines whether you're a threat to her. Frankly, the family has given me the authority to do whatever I think best about you. Who knows? I might decide in your favor."

"My objective is to meet my half sister and give her a message. I'd like to learn a little about her, too, because I don't have any brothers or sisters except her, and I learned about her only a few months ago. But if I can only give her the message, that'll be enough."

"I could pass this mysterious message along."

"No. I want to meet her myself." Rebecca looked at him

pensively. "The message is from my—that is, *our*—father."

"Who is now deceased, I understand."

She nodded. A twinge of grief made her look away; she felt exposed and vulnerable. "He died last April."

"And your mother?"

"She died when I was a child."

"And so you're all alone, and perhaps in need of money? Is that why you came to Thailand on this strange mission of yours?"

Because she'd been raised to hold her temper, she stifled an urge to hit him with her satchel. Instead she rose sternly, tossed the satchel onto his desk, along with her purse, and stood facing him with her hands clasped behind her back. "You don't even know me," she said in a slow, even voice that shook with anger. "I don't need any money. I didn't come here to get money. I came here to meet my blood relative and tell her about our father. I've brought pictures of him, mementoes, things I thought she ought to see."

Kash silently congratulated her on her dignity. He slid forward on the plush sofa and steepled his hands under his chin, never taking his eyes off her. In her white blouse and skirt she stood out among the dark office colors. The lamps lit her dramatically, bringing something unfathomable to her smooth, pretty face. He held his breath, studying her. There was a timeless quality about her that made him think of a classic painting. Something basic and strong. A man could read an infinite number of interpretations into her, and find something new each time.

There was nothing remarkable about her—no heart-stopping beauty in her face, no extraordinary curves under her neat and proper clothes, but she was, nonetheless, fascinating. Something about that open, utterly uninhibited smile she'd given him at first, he thought. Or maybe it was just that her act was so good, so—he searched for a word to describe her—so *whole-some.*

"How old are you?" he asked abruptly. "In comparison to Ms. Vatan, I mean."

"I'm three years younger than she is. Twenty-six," she said sharply. "Wait a minute—don't change the subject. About my money situation, I'm not rolling in gold, but I have a comfortable income. In case none of your people have told you yet, I draw cartoons for a living. I'm good at what I do, and I have a syndicated strip that runs in papers all over the Midwest. So I didn't come here to mooch off the Vatan family." She started toward her satchel. "I brought a sample."

He stood and raised a hand. She halted. "I've seen your work. The sample you left with Mr. Prasartthong at the Vatan offices. Your work is unique."

Unique? Rebecca thought with annoyance. The way he said it, it wasn't much of a compliment.

"I only glanced at the cartoons," he confessed, cocking a brow at her and smiling slightly. "I'm not a good judge of such things."

"Are you a good judge of people?"

"Yes."

"Then why don't you give me a chance?" She gestured toward herself with outspread hands. "I don't dress like a minister's old-maid daughter so people will think I'm a sexy, dangerous babe in disguise."

For the first time he laughed. Rebecca listened closely to the low, throaty sound and found it both sinister and erotic. Her skin absorbed it and tingled. He walked toward her, and she stood rooted in place, even when tiny muscles in her stomach were quivering in resistance.

He halted close enough to touch her. She dropped her hands to her sides, realizing that they gave the impression of reaching for him. But she gazed up at him without wavering. His eyes were the color of dark honey, shadowed by thick black lashes that curled up at the tips. She found herself mesmerized by those soft, curving lashes, which were so out of place among the harder lines of his face.

That face held emotions she couldn't decipher, and his own silent scrutiny of her made the tension worse. She rarely wore makeup other than a dab of lipstick and eye shadow, and didn't worry about the effect. No one had ever called her ugly, and if men didn't beat a path to her door, well, she didn't want them crowding her doormat anyway. She had more important concerns, like making a living. Thousands of people tried to sell cartoons; only the most dedicated were successful.

But Kashadlin Santelli's shrewd, overtly masculine attention made her want to touch her face and discover what fascinated him, whether it was good or bad. "I'll find out *exactly* who and what you are," he told her. "And I hope you're what you claim to be."

She exhaled roughly. "I am."

"A minister's old-maid daughter? Is that what you are?"

"That's part of what I am, sort of. Yes, my dad was a Methodist minister. A retired army chaplain. When he was in the army, he was stationed in Thailand for several years. Back in the early sixties."

"So that's where your bizarre story begins."

"Bizarre? At least you didn't call it 'insane,' which is what one of the Vatan executives said. I'm progressing."

"You're aware, of course, that Ms. Vatan's father was a British Army Officer who was killed in a military accident not long after her mother died?"

"I'm aware that everyone believes that story, but it's not true."

"Because your father, a retired army chaplain in Iowa, told you a different story, about the heiress of a very well known Thai silk company?"

Rebecca leaned toward him, clenching her fists at her sides. "Because when he was dying, my father told me

about his first wife and their daughter, whom he loved
very much. He wasn't the kind of man who lied."

"Only the kind of man who could desert his Thai wife
and daughter then?"

"He didn't desert them!" she said loudly. Kashadlin
Santelli didn't blink, though she was inches from his
face. She realized how close she was, and how hard her
heart was pounding. "His wife died, and her family took
the baby. He was never able to get her back. Because he
was a foreigner, he had no rights."

"So he waited all these years to mention this lost
daughter to you. Why?"

"That's for me to discuss with my half sister."

Kash's fascination with her turned to anger. It was
time to stop the charade. "No, that's for you to discuss
with me. If I think there's any merit in your story, I'll
report it to her."

"Then I'll stay in Thailand until I find her myself."

"With the help of your employers?"

"My what?" She stared at him openmouthed.

He grabbed her by the wrists and pinned her arms
against his chest. In one swift, graceful move he backed
her against his massive desk. She stumbled and sat
down on the beveled edge. It pressed into her hips,
while his fingers pressed into her arms. Her shout of
shock broke off in speechless disbelief as he trapped her
with his body. Her precarious balance made her struggle for a foothold; one foot was drawn up, the other
slipping on the sleek tapestry rug under the desk. He
pressed tightly against her from chest to thigh, with her
legs splayed around him. Rebecca's skirt bunched up
between her thighs but was barely a cushion for his
lower body. His hipbones pressed hard against her soft
flesh.

"Be still," he ordered mildly. "I simply want you to pay
attention to what I'm about to say."

"Where I come from, a man doesn't assault a woman
to make her listen to him."

"If this were an assault, it would clearly be painful. I haven't hurt you. In fact, I guarantee that I won't hurt you. Which is more than you can promise me about your intentions."

"I have no intentions other than to meet my half sister!"

"You work for the Nalinat family. Admit it."

"I never heard of them! Let go of me!"

"You're not in America. There's no place to run to, no one to call for help. If you want to be trusted, you'll have to trust me, believe every word I tell you." He bent his head closer, and his dark eyes bored into hers without blinking. "Ms. Vatan had no American army chaplain for a father. She and her relatives have said so, and that's why no one will allow you to see her. There's no point. We know you're lying."

"No. I don't understand why no one will agree with my story, but it's true."

"You're working for the Nalinats. If not, then you're a fool for stepping into the middle of a very ugly feud between them and the Vatan family."

Furious, she struggled against him. "I wish I knew who these Nalinats are! I'd love to know something that's supposed to be so important to me!"

He pulled her tighter against him. "Calmly, calmly," he commanded. Kash saw the blazing disgust in her eyes. He searched for fear, for lies, also, but found only the fury. He'd already noticed too much that had nothing to do with his work—the opalescent flecks in their blue background, the seductive way the dark brown lashes swept down at the outer corners.

"I know what the Nalinats are trying to accomplish," he told her. "I just don't know what part you play in it. But whatever they're paying you, it isn't worth it. This feud is over. Mayura Vatan will never marry their son, no matter how much the Nalinats threaten or harass her. Now why don't you pack your bags and go back to Iowa—or wherever you're from."

"Tell Mayura Vatan that her half sister is staying in Thailand until she agrees to meet me! I think I can prove the truth, but I'm not going to try with anyone but her. I don't know anything about this family feud. I swear!"

"If you stay and if you cause trouble, you'll answer to me."

"What kind of threat is that?"

Kash debated for a moment. It only mattered that she believe him capable of carrying out his threats, not whether he could stoop so low. "Do you know what can happen to a woman alone in Bangkok? The pleasure trades are not discriminating about the strangers they absorb. People disappear here—they're sold, bought, or simply bartered for more valuable goods. If you cause me trouble, I'll make certain you spend the rest of your life in a manner you don't want to imagine."

Her sharp gasp gave him a sense of victory, but at the same time he regretted it. What if she was telling the truth? *You were hired to protect Mayura Vatan, not this stranger,* he reminded himself.

"You sound like a B-movie villain," she said bitterly, though her voice shook a little. "I haven't done anything wrong, and if you try to hurt me, you'll get more than you bargained for."

"Hurt?" he repeated, smiling harshly. She didn't give up. Her bluster was impressive. "I told you I wouldn't hurt you. There are ways to make a woman behave that have nothing to do with pain."

He closed his mouth over hers in a taunting kiss, catching her when her lips were half-open. Kash felt the stiffening of her body in rejection at the same time that the sweet softness of her mouth exploded in his senses.

She couldn't want him to kiss her. He knew that. He didn't expect to feel anything himself, as he twisted against her and her hands sank into his coat sleeves, tugging fiercely. But for one shattering moment he wasn't trying to make a point and she wasn't trying to resist. For one instant the kiss was a heated caress, as shocking as the thoughts that cascaded through his mind in an angry, urgent chant.

Be who you say you are, Rebecca Brown. Be some-one special. Please. I want to know what you are, everything you are.

Suddenly she clamped her mouth shut and wrenched her head away. He saw her stunned expression and flushed skin; he heard the splintered panting of her breath, and his own. He knew why he was upset. He didn't like the effect she had on him, the element of desire that lay underneath the tension. He was wary of her.

But she was terrified of him. He saw that in her wide-eyed stare, the way it remained frozen on him, as if she was desperately trying to guard herself against whatever he would do next. Her hands were shaking so hard that he felt the tremors through his clothes.

Kash looked down at her in speechless realization. He'd never forced a woman to kiss him before. He'd never caused one to fear him physically. For someone with his background to play this kind of game was beyond excuse.

Self-rebuke shot through him so strongly that his stomach twisted with nausea. He let go of Rebecca Brown and stepped back. Being turned loose caught her off guard. She nearly toppled off the desk.

"We'll meet again, unless you leave the country," he told her in a brusque voice. "You don't want to meet me again."

"I don't want to even *think* about you again." She grabbed her satchel and purse, then shook out her skirt with a violent motion of one hand. Her blue eyes glittered. Even her shoulder-length brown hair seemed to be quivering. "But I'm not leaving Thailand until I meet my half sister."

Kash cursed under his breath, but her anger reassured him. He'd rather have her angry at him than afraid. He wished she were telling the truth. Rebecca

Brown, successful cartoonist, minister's daughter, self-proclaimed old maid, and corn-fed wholesome Iowa princess, ought to be for real. The world needed more ordinary, likable people. But there was nothing ordinary about the recklessness she brought out in him.

"You've picked your fight," he said, as she brushed past him and went to the doors. "I only hope you change your mind quickly."

She opened the door and halted, drawing herself up with dignity as she looked back at him. "When I came here to find Mayura Vatan, I decided to take chances and do things I've never done before." She gave him a bewildered, somewhat despairing once-over. "I thought I'd fall in love with Thailand. I have. But I never expected to find so much ugliness here. You personify it."

He bowed sardonically and pressed his hands together in a *wai* as she shut the door softly behind her. But her words lingered, and troubled him.

Two

Rebecca put the finishing touches on a wicked cartoon drawing of Kashadlin Santelli. She'd sketched him on a hotel notepad, while soaking in the bathtub with a hot towel wedged behind her neck. In her drawing he was a fanged dragon in a tailored suit, with a long, scaly tail curled around him. Scribbling violently, she filled in the dragon's eyes so they'd have the appropriate dark glare to them.

The phone rang as she was toweling herself off. Rebecca heard it vaguely, not only because her hearing aid lay on the bedside table but because her thoughts were still on her dragon. Glancing at herself in the dresser mirror on her way to the phone, she noted the excited flush on her face and breasts. Rebecca groaned silently in self-rebuke and wrapped the towel around her slender torso. All right, so there was something a little exhilarating about the memory of being grabbed and kissed by him. Dragons were in short supply in Iowa.

"You ought to be ashamed," she muttered at herself as well as him, as she picked up the phone. "Hello?"

"Hello," answered a pleasant female voice with a Thai accent. "Ms. Brown?"

"Yes."

"This is Mayura Vatan. I'm sorry for all you've been through. I think it's time we met."

After a speechless second Rebecca asked numbly, "Are you really Mayura? I'm sorry, but I've been misled a lot during the past two weeks."

"I assure you, I'm real."

"But I thought there was no chance of my seeing you."

"I'm afraid we Thais are a little suspicious of foreigners. But I'm intrigued by your story. I've never known much about my parents. I don't see how you and I could be related, but I'd like to talk with you."

Rebecca sighed in relief. "Mr. Santelli must have decided to trust me."

For a moment there was only silence. Then the caller said, "Why, yes."

Even though Santelli's change of heart was bewildering, Rebecca silently thanked him. Perhaps she'd give the dragon a smile. "I can't wait to meet you!" she said to Mayura.

"Nor I, you. Come to the Farang Restaurant. The hotel people can tell you how to find it. In about an hour?"

"Yes! Thank you!"

Rebecca dressed in a pinstriped summer dress of white and blue, pulled a thin white jacket over it, and spit-polished her white flats. She considered her modest, ordinary clothes no more a reflection of her personality than her hearing aid. She might be conservative, but not narrow-minded. From her father she'd learned not to judge people by their looks, and that included herself. Shooting a hard glance at the dragon cartoon she'd tossed on the bed, she decided that Kashadlin Santelli's stunning physical appeal and beautiful clothes were proof that appearances could be deceptive. Inside, he was a big, cold-blooded lizard.

Around her neck she put a thin gold chain and caressed the small pendant, a faded and scratched cloisonné lotus blossom. It was one of two pieces of jewelry belonging to Mayura's mother. Rebecca's father had saved them for almost thirty years. He'd given both to Rebecca only a few days before he died. They weren't valuable except for the sentiment, but they were Rebecca's only real hope of convincing Mayura Vatan of the truth. She hadn't shown them to anyone else because she'd wanted to share them first with her half sister. That sentiment had cost her time and trouble, she knew, but now it would be repaid.

The other piece of jewelry, an earring, was in the hotel safe. On her way out Rebecca almost stopped and requested it, but a cautious inner voice made her change her mind.

Halfway to the restaurant, as she bounced in the passenger seat of a sputtering *tuk tuk*, she realized she'd forgotten her satchel containing photos of her father. He'd had no pictures of himself with Mayura or her mother, but Rebecca had hoped the photos of him would show his and Mayura's resemblance. Rebecca decided to go on without them; with any luck, this would only be her first meeting with her half sister. There'd be time later for sharing everything else.

On a street filled with elegant shops and eateries, most with signs in both English and Thai, the *tuk tuk* driver stopped in front of a pagodalike building. Traffic, as usual, streamed around him in an impatient rush, and the sidewalks were full of many foreigners like herself, a clean-cut tourist crowd. "Hurry, please," the driver warned, smiling. "Or we'll be pushed aside like an ant."

Laughing, Rebecca handed him a generous number of bills as she got out. "Ms. Brown?" someone called. She turned quickly and saw a uniformed Thai chauffeur waiting beside a long black limousine, which had just pulled up behind the *tuk tuk*. "Yes?"

He gestured toward the passenger door he'd opened. "Please. Miss Vatan is here."

Rebecca hurried over, smiling, thinking that finally

things were looking up, and maybe the dragon, Santelli, really was softhearted to have arranged this meeting. Then the chauffeur shoved her headfirst into the limo's backseat and a pair of men dragged her between them, each holding one of her arms in brutal grips. A hand was clamped over her mouth, and she saw the flash of a long silver knife as it came to rest in warning against her throat. The chauffeur shut the door calmly, and the limo's tinted windows blocked out the rest of the world. Rebecca thought her lungs would burst from holding back a scream.

"We'd like to have your cooperation," one of the men said pleasantly. "So we won't have to hurt you."

As the car pulled away from the curb, one black thought rose up through her fear and shock over being tricked. *Never trust a dragon.*

Stretched out facedown on the soft, thick Oriental rug on his apartment floor, wearing only a black towel, which was draped across his hips, Kash tried to relax and clear his mind of Rebecca Brown. His very pregnant, very beautiful Thai masseuse chatted about her husband and family while her hands pounded on a tight knot of muscle in his right shoulder. Her blouse and baggy trousers occasionally brushed his bare skin as she bent over him, her knees sunk into a sumptuous throw pillow.

Kash listened distractedly, his head resting on his folded arms, his eyes shut. He told himself that Rebecca Brown shouldn't stick in his mind this way, like a slow, sexy dream from which he was reluctant to wake. She was so ordinary—only a little taller than average, a little prettier than average, a little better at hiding her real goals behind an act. But everything added up to something unique. Maybe the secret was that disarming grin she'd given him, that unselfconscious openness.

Kash frowned. *But she's hiding behind a facade. You believe that. You are convinced of it, aren't you?*

"Stop thinking, please," his masseuse ordered mildly in Thai. "Your muscles are fighting me. Life was meant to be enjoyed. What occupies your mind so much?"

"A woman," Kash said dourly.

She laughed. "A man like you must have more women in his bed—and inside his head—than he needs."

"Of course."

Kash wondered if she'd be disappointed to know the truth. People who didn't know him well assumed he had a new woman in his bed each night. To them his dark good looks, wealth, and sophistication added up to a lusty lifestyle. But the people closest to him—and there were only a handful besides Audubon—knew that he spent most of his time alone. Kash brooded sometimes over the difference in his image and the reality. But from his childhood, he'd learned the alternative to being too defensive about intimacy was to become brutally insensitive. He preferred loneliness to that.

He rubbed his forehead, feeling the throbbing in his temples. Thailand stirred up old memories of Vietnam, where, thirty years ago, he'd been born, and where he'd spent the first eight years of his life. On his mother's side he was one-fourth Vietnamese and one-fourth Egyptian; on his father's he was half American. He'd never known his biological father. His adopted father, Audubon, loved him and was loved in return, but even the powerful and wealthy Audubon couldn't change some of life's crueler realities.

After the masseuse left, he placed a call to Audubon, in Virginia. His father's longtime assistant, Clarice, quizzed him about his eating habits, whether or not he was behaving himself, and generally treated him as she always had, as if he were still the stony-faced eight-year-old who'd arrived in Audubon's home straight from the streets of Saigon, in great need of a motherly person to order him around.

Smiling, he affectionately chided her for talking about personal subjects when they were supposed to be conducting business. His father's highly organized network of private security people owed its smooth communications to her, but he enjoyed teasing her, and she enjoyed telling him to mind his elders.

"Audubon and Elena are in Richmond at the symphony," Clarice said. "But I can page him. Is it urgent?"

Kash smiled to himself in approval. His adoptive father, now happily married after many years of devoting himself to his unique security service, deserved the privacy and leisure. "No, I only wanted to discuss tactics with him. It can wait. Give him and Elena my love. And if you don't mind, start checking background on someone for me."

"I live to serve, boy," Clarice said with her cheeky Texas twang. "Who's the subject?"

He told her all he knew about Rebecca Brown. Clarice sniffed smugly. "If she's for real, I'll find out."

"She may be for real, but she may also be working for the Nalinats."

"Have a little faith, Kash. Some people *are* what they seem to be."

He was debating that philosophy seconds later when the phone rang. Kash listened to his Thai assistant, who'd been instructed to follow Rebecca Brown any time she left her hotel. When the man told Kash where the intrepid Ms. Brown and her mysterious escorts had gone, and that she hadn't gone willingly, he was bewildered. He dressed quickly, almost jerking on his clothes in haste. A surprising sense of protectiveness shot through him, along with some guilt. Only *he* had the right to torment Rebecca Brown.

"What do you want from Mayura Vatan?" the wiry man demanded again.

"Nothing," Rebecca said grimly. Now that they'd taken

the blindfold off, her gaze darted to the walls of the tiny room. They were covered in red velvet and painted with gaudy murals of men and women making love in a variety of badly painted but explicit positions. Her stomach twisted in disgust at the raw sleaziness of the room, with its smell of stale incense, its faded couch and battered table, and most of all the squeaky bed with its bare mattress. She sat as close to the edge as she could. They'd tied her hands behind her and her feet to the bed's foot. The man who kept asking her questions was seated close beside her. He smelled of sweat and fish. The other man sat on the couch, twirling the knife in one hand.

This was the last straw. She didn't know where she was, or who they were, or what might happen next. But they worked for Kashadlin Santelli, and she'd rather suffer than cooperate with *him*.

The man beside her ripped the necklace off. She sucked in a sharp breath as pain zipped along the back of her neck. "This is Thai workmanship," the man said in heavily accented English. "Where did you get it?"

"The jewelry section at the five-and-dime in Dubuque, Iowa."

The men traded puzzled, then angry, looks. "You are related to the Vatan family," the one with the knife accused.

She stared at him in disbelief. First Kashadlin Santelli had insisted she worked for the Nalinat family, whoever they were, and now this greasy pair had abducted her because they thought she was part of the Vatan family.

Rebecca's mind whirled with confusion and fear. "I'm a cartoonist." There. That's telling 'em, she thought weakly.

"You know where Mayura Vatan has gone."

"No."

"You'll tell us where she is. You've been telling people that she's your sister."

"Half sister. I don't *know* where she is. I thought your boss realized that." She spat out the name with contempt. "Mr. Santelli."

The men traded blank looks. She was more bewildered. "You tell us where she is!" the man with the knife shouted. He came over and knelt in front of her. "You tell, or you'll be sorry."

She felt icy perspiration on her forehead as she stared at the blade. "I'm already sorry. Sorry your mother had children." She tried to laugh, but the sound trailed off in breathless horror.

He put the knife tip in the center of her scoop-necked bodice, snagged a bit of material, and sliced upward in one neat stroke. Rebecca's blood froze, but her heart was pumping wildly. She could either make a joke or faint. "I always . . . wanted a plunging . . . neckline on this dress," she managed to say.

"You're in a pleasure house," the man told her, his eyes glinting with victory. "We'll show you exactly what that means."

For the second time she thought about screaming, for whatever good it would do. But suddenly loud footsteps sounded in the outer hall, and someone knocked fervently. The men leaped to open the room's door. A woman spoke to them in rapid Thai, wringing her hands. Rebecca craned her head at the squeals and protests coming from elsewhere in the house, running feet, and men's voices speaking in fluid Thai, which she couldn't understand at all.

Her captors shoved the door wide open and bounded out, apparently escaping in the opposite direction. She gazed wide-eyed at the doorway and waited with dread. Whoever had arrived might be worse.

Soon footsteps came down the hall. Her heart froze as Kashadlin Santelli filled the doorway. He wore only black slacks and a gray dress shirt, with the collar open and sleeves rolled up. He looked casual except for the gleaming black pistol in one hand and the expression of stark concentration on his face. When he saw her, his intense gaze flickered over her with disbelief, and a second later, darkened with fury.

Rebecca watched him warily, every nerve on edge. She'd given up trying to understand what anyone wanted or suspected, but she didn't doubt that this man was no less an enemy than the men who'd kidnapped her.

"Playing both sides can get you in serious trouble," he said sternly, but the puzzlement in his eyes softened the taunt. He came to her in two long, graceful strides and knelt in front of her. Other men were running down the hall after her abductors.

"You did this," she accused, her voice shaking with fury. "You did this to me."

"No."

"You said you would."

"I didn't do this." He tucked the gun under his belt and leaned half across her, angling his body so he could reach around her. She was engulfed in the curve of his body, as if he were hugging her. She turned her head to escape looking at him. His cheek was close to hers. His scent was warm and sweaty. The cool Mr. Santelli had actually gone to the trouble of exerting himself to find her. For what reason?

His hands closed over the tape that bound her wrists. He ripped it with a strength that made her jump. "Sorry," he said brusquely, working at the tape. "Are you hurt?"

"What kind of charade is this?" She gulped for breath and to keep from crying in sheer frustration. "You order two cavemen to maul me, then you show up for some kind of rescue."

"Dammit, that isn't how I operate, Ms. Brown." He leaned back after he'd freed her hands. Bringing them around to her lap, he rubbed the irritated skin on her wrists while he frowned at her harshly. "Believe me, I didn't order anyone to kidnap you."

"Then how did you know I was here?"

"I had you followed. Lucky for you."

"Why should I believe you?" She jerked her hands away.

He licked his forefinger and reached forward. Before she could pull back, she felt his wet fingertip stroking a spot on the side of her neck. It stung, but the moisture was soothing. "You're bleeding," he said gruffly. Either there was true concern in his voice, or her hearing aid was acting up. She blamed the hearing aid.

"They stole my necklace." Rebecca looked hard into his eyes, while surprise grew inside her. Despite her anger, she was starting to feel relieved. Safe. Rescued. By him. The dragon who had hinted that he'd do something as terrible as this to her if she stayed in Thailand. So why was he gently smoothing his finger over her scraped skin?

"They're not working for me," he said grimly. He sat back on his heels and began unfastening the rope around her ankles. "Or for the Vatan family."

"Nothing makes any sense. They accused me of being part of the Vatan family!"

He went still. His eyes searched hers. "You're making enemies you didn't expect to make. Perhaps if you tell me the truth about your reasons for being here, I could help you discover why those men wanted you."

"I've told you the truth!" As he freed her feet, she pushed herself back on the dirty mattress and glared at him bitterly. "Just leave me alone."

"If I granted that wish, you'd be worse off than you know. Think what might have happened to you tonight if I hadn't had someone following you."

She looked down at herself and the gaping bodice of her dress. The knife had sliced her slip as well. Her breasts, small but full, strained against the exposed cups of her bra. "Are you injured there?" Santelli asked bluntly. Before she realized what he intended, he reached over and spread the cut material with his fingers, brushing the inside curves of her breasts above the bra. He studied them with poker-faced calm, his dark gaze moving slowly.

His scrutiny burned her as much as the touch of his fingers had. Grinding her teeth in confusion over his tenderness, Rebecca grabbed his large hands and pushed them away. "Maybe I ought to scream for the Sleaze Brothers to come back. At least they didn't hide their nastier impulses behind a gallant show."

Santelli's eyes rose to hers. The cold warning in his gaze sent a shiver down her spine. "You know far more about hiding ugly impulses than I do, Ms. Brown. I've told you nothing but facts. You've told me nothing but an outrageous story about being my client's half sister. You may be nothing but a bald-faced con artist hoping to worm your way into a wealthy Thai family."

"Mr. Santelli, get away from me and get out of this room. I'd rather talk to the crummiest customer in this brothel than continue this conversation with you."

He made his voice sound prim. "Gee, lady, the last time I heard someone described as 'crummy,' I was no more than twelve years old and watching an episode of *Leave It to Beaver*."

She felt her face begin to burn with embarrassment as well as anger. "I don't have to describe a pig wallow in pig language."

"I suppose that's my cue to oink."

"It's your cue to leave. I'll take care of myself now. I don't need you or your attitude toward me. I'm not accustomed to men who think I'm capable of immoral and even criminal intentions. I won't put up with it. When you find out how wrong you are about me, I hope you're ashamed of yourself for accusing me. *Get out*."

Kash gave into an urge to keep taunting her, to expose her for whoever and whatever she really was. He said tautly, "I haven't been scolded so, ummm, grandly, in years and never with such an air of wounded innocence. I'll grant you one thing—if this Goody Two-shoes attitude is an act, you've mastered it."

Rebecca's eyes narrowed fiercely. A sharp sound of rage burst from her throat. "You want to see how crazy you can make a Goody Two-shoes? How you can turn a peaceful, polite person into a maniac? Fine!" She shoved him hard. "Get out!" His taut, thick shoulder muscles flexed powerfully, but the rest of him didn't budge.

"Calm down," he said in a tightly controlled voice. Kash bit the inside of his cheek. Her righteous nonsense had worn thin. "At the moment I don't care whether you're an angel or not. Unless you're damned good at surviving in the wildest section of one of the most notorious cities in the world, you need me. A woman like you wouldn't get far on the street."

She shoved him again. "Read my lips. *I don't need your help. Leave.*"

"I don't like violence. Or naive stupidity. Stop it."

Rebecca had never struck a person in anger before, not even as a child, but she drew back a fist and punched him in the chest. It wasn't a coy tap; it was a roundhouse slug, and it made a deep *whump*.

Santelli's reaction was fast, so fast that she guessed he had trained reflexes that could have easily warded off her punch, if he'd wanted to. He sprang forward, encircled her in his arms, and flattened her on the bare gray mattress. Her feet dangled on the floor. One of his went between them, accompanied, farther up, by his leg. She felt his knee settle between her own, at the mattress's edge. The rest of him lay intimately on top of her.

His face was livid. She glared up into his eyes and was frozen by their intense emotions. Their directness mesmerized her.

"You are *not* as tough as you think you are," he told her, speaking in a low, fierce voice. "And regardless of whether you despise me or not, I'm the only help you have right now. You can't wear your respectable little

Sunday-school manners like a badge and assume they'll scare off the rest of the world."

She writhed under him, but his weight held her down. "I don't need this kind of help."

"You may not have noticed, Ms. Brown, but you've got a female body. That alone is enough to get you in serious trouble in this part of Bangkok. Unfortunately, your particular female body is attractive and comes with a pretty face. There are plenty of men who'd pay to have you on this bed wearing nothing but your exceptionally smooth pink hide, Ms. Brown, and they wouldn't care if you wanted to be here, or not. They wouldn't even care if you were conscious. You're in luck, because as unpleasant and dastardly as you think I am, I'm not that kind of man. But believe me, my annoying, ignorant Ms. Brown, I know all about brothels and what happens to people in them. Now will you quit fighting me and cooperate in getting yourself out of here?"

She felt muscles straining in her neck. She realized that she had bared her teeth at him. He'd nearly reduced her to snarling, like a cornered cat. Her violent reactions to him frightened her a little. Rebecca licked her lips and tried to speak in a calm voice. "I'll do anything that will keep you from mashing me to death or giving me another lecture."

"Is that a yes?"

"*Yes.*"

He let go of her abruptly and, breathing lightly, rolled off her and sat up. She frowned at him thoughtfully as she sat up also. She put a clammy hand over her torn dress, picturing the red marks his shirt buttons must have pressed into her breasts.

"Here," Santelli said, now using a gruff, sympathetic tone. She refused to acknowledge him as he unbuttoned his shirt and removed it. He draped it around her shoulders. Wordlessly she grasped the sides and pulled them closed. Her gaze was drawn rebelliously to his bare chest. It was no less beautiful than she'd imagined—

golden and muscular, with fine, curly black hair. She looked away hurriedly, even though she knew her staring had been obvious.

"It's perfectly all right," he said quaintly. "You can admire mine, since I've already admired *yours*." His tone was so exaggerated that she broke into a weary laugh. He lifted one of her hands to his chest, held it flat against the furry, warm surface, then pushed it away dramatically. "Stop that," he said deadpan. "Stop, or I'll scream."

She laughed again and, bending forward, put her head in her hands. The laugh trailed off into a hiccup, then a soft sound of distress. He stroked her shoulder.

"I only want to meet Mayura Vatan," she said doggedly. "If I have to hire my own bodyguard, I will. You can think whatever you want to about me. I don't trust you any more than you trust me. But if you really had nothing to do with this incident tonight, then I appreciate your getting me out of it."

"How did they hurt your neck?"

"They tore my necklace off."

"Do you have any idea why?"

"If I did, I wouldn't tell you." She slid to one side to avoid him, then pushed herself off the bed. Standing shakily, she remembered through a dull fog of shock that they'd tossed her purse in one corner. She stumbled and braced her hand on the wall as she bent to retrieve it. It was empty; she thought of her passport, traveler's checks, and wallet, the extra battery for her hearing aid, her small notepad with its sketches of Thai scenes, her Thai phrase book. For the first time she felt alone and helpless in an alien place. "It's all gone," she said in soft anguish. "Everything that makes me feel safe is gone."

Sickly pinpoints of light burst in front of her eyes. She stumbled. Abruptly Santelli was in front of her, picking up the purse. He took her firmly by one arm as she straightened.

"After what you've been through, you're allowed a little wooziness," he said.

"I'm not a fainter, just a stumbler. Stumbling is part of my personality."

"You're good at it, then."

"Let go of my arm."

"You'll fall down. I'd rather you not pass out in this particular establishment. Have a little class, Ms. Brown. Pass out in a better grade of brothel."

His teasing was unexpected and absurdly effective. Her head cleared a little. "*Brothel* is such a quaint, old-fashioned word."

"There's nothing quaint about it. I can be blunt, if you want."

"No need. I'm well aware of what goes on in places like this."

"Oh?" He was holding her up with his grip on her arm but also with his throaty, taunting tone. "How would you know?"

"Even in Iowa, we're hip to decadence."

"Hip to decadence? I think not, Ms. Brown. You haven't the faintest idea." She blinked at him. "Bad choice of words," he amended, frowning. "Don't faint."

"I'm not a fainter, I told you."

"As soon as your face is more pink than white, I'll take you outside." He gently pushed her against a wall. She leaned gratefully. "Breathe. Slowly."

Rebecca focused on his face, but looking up at him only made her head swim. He was one tall, gorgeous mystery, and she was going crazy trying to decide how dangerous he was. Her gaze flicked past him to the lurid wall paintings.

"Well, something is making you pink again, thank God," he said sardonically. Following her line of vision, he glanced over at the wall. For several seconds they studied the paintings in silence. She was too numb to be embarrassed, titillated, or even disgusted. "Some of those positions look uncomfortable," she heard herself say. "And I suspect the proportions are all wrong." She didn't believe her own mouth, but she must be speaking, because he shot her a startled look.

He cleared his throat and said solemnly, "Exaggeration makes for good erotica but bad self-comparison."

"Exaggeration makes for a big ego."

"There are some large egos in these paintings, then."

"Male egos," she said dryly.

"Yes, these were probably painted by a man."

"This is a man's place," she agreed, looking around. "The women are only property."

"This is not a man's place," he corrected, with an odd edge in his voice. "It's where the filth of the world settles to the bottom. Come on, let's get out of here."

His vivid distaste for the brothel struck her as respectable. A man who disliked brothels couldn't be all bad. *Some compliment*, she thought grimly. Still, she voluntarily wobbled along beside him up a hallway where Thai women—some of them no more than girls— peeked out of doorways. Some wore only panties, and a couple wore less than that. Rebecca couldn't think of anything better to do, so she smiled at them and nodded politely. They smiled and nodded back. "You're an extraordinarily friendly person," Santelli said drolly. "None of them would have lifted a finger to stop what was happening to you."

"They're afraid. I can see it in their eyes. They probably do what they're told."

"You're right. I'm impressed with your intuition." He added silently, *And your compassion.*

"You never accused me of being callous, remember? Just naive and stupid."

"You must be feeling better. You're recovering that wicked Iowa wit."

Outside, in an alley strewn with garbage, he guided her toward a large dark sedan of some European make. Rebecca took a deep breath of hot night air and stopped. "What makes you think I'll get into that car with you?"

Two well-dressed but disheveled Thai men rounded a distant corner in the alley and came toward them. Rebecca took a wary step back. "They're my assistants," Santelli said quickly. "Relax."

"They're big enough to be Sumo wrestlers."

"Sumo wrestlers are Japanese, not Thai."

"They should move to Japan."

"Please get in the car. You can't wait on the street for a taxi. You're in one of the seediest sections of the city. I'll take you back to your hotel room. Look, Ms. Brown, I've already passed up my chance to ravish you, so put your mind at ease."

"Around you? Forget it."

"The lady has a sharp wit, but she's leaning toward the car. A good sign. Look, her feet are moving when I push her a little. She refuses to speak, but she's agreeing to my wishes. For once, she's cooperating. Amazing."

By the time he finished badgering her, he had the car's back passenger door open, and she was wearily nodding her consent. It hardly seemed likely that he'd saved her from something treacherous just to harm her himself. At least, not tonight.

When she was seated on the plush cushions, he leaned in and brushed her bangs back from her forehead. Rebecca shot him a rebuking look, but it faded when she saw the admiration in his eyes. Quickly he pulled his hand back, and his eyes became shuttered. "I'll be right back," he told her. Then, adding a slight, mocking smile, "With my Sumo wrestlers in tow."

When they arrived at her hotel, one of Bangkok's modern, Western-style high rises, she sighed with relief. For the moment her notions of adventure were dulled with the knowledge that her life was tangled with that of Kashadlin Santelli, a man who'd made her feel furious, afraid, excited, and safe—all in the first day she'd known him. After covering his torso in a loose cotton undershirt he'd borrowed from one of his assistants, he accompanied her to her room with the calm, confident air of a man who considered the day pretty ordinary. For someone such as him, it probably was.

Her head throbbed with fatigue, and each time she glanced at Santelli during their walk down the hall to her room, she had the light-headed sensation of whirling in place. She was involved with the most exotic, intriguing, but antagonizing man on this or any continent. Her exhausted mind sluggishly tried to understand him, and failed. Even her vivid imagination failed her. She struggled to picture what might happen next between her and Santelli. Probably full-scale war.

But when she stepped into her room and flicked on the light, he was the one who cursed softly on her behalf, expressing the shock that left her speechless. Dresser drawers hung open. A chair was overturned. There was no sign of the clothes or other belongings she'd left scattered around the room.

The absurdity of the day's bad luck made her give a short, anguished laugh. "Pardon me for asking, Mr. Santelli," she said finally, "but did you have me robbed?" Kash looked heavenward and simply shook his head. She nodded. "I'm going to take a big leap of faith and believe you."

Kash put a hand over his heart. "The world just stopped turning," he said, deadpan. "Oh, how can I ever thank you for this honor?"

"Do you believe in fate?" she asked, staring up at him glumly.

"Yes."

"Then I think you're stuck with me. I'm not budging until I find out who did this."

He sighed grandly. "You've sealed your destiny." The words rang true to him, more than he'd admit.

Three

Kash fought a strong desire to put his arm around her. Whatever her deceptions, right now she was undeniably forlorn as she walked to the center of her room. Turning in a slow circle, she pointed to the neatly made bed. "I left my satchel there with the pictures of my father inside." Then she gestured at the top of the sleek, contemporary dresser. "My green scarf was there. And a little jade Buddha I bought from a street vendor."

With his shirt hanging on her slender body like a tent, and her glossy brunette hair raggedly pushed back from her ashen face, Kash could believe she was a harmless, helpless tourist, and a very innocent one. He subdued the sentimental idea and reminded himself that he had a lot to learn about her before he'd consider giving up his suspicions. Her story about being Mayura Vatan's half sister had no supporting evidence, plus Mayura's five aunts and uncles had provided Kash with photos and letters of the British officer who had been Mayura's father.

"Ms. Brown?" he called softly. She was so distracted that she didn't hear. "Rebecca?" he amended, liking the gentle sound of it.

She lifted surprised eyes to him. "Yes?"

"If the men who kidnapped you and did this to your room work for the Nalinat family, it's a point in your favor. You're obviously not spying for them."

"Oh? So instead of accusing me of spying on Mayura Vatan, you're now just accusing me of being a con artist who wants to wrangle money from her?"

"We're making progress, at least."

Kash frowned as he watched Rebecca walk woodenly toward the bathroom. He stopped her and went in first. It was empty. When he waved her in, his discovery must have shown in his face, because she mumbled, "Don't tell me they took everything in there too." He could see her distressed blue eyes focus blankly on the marble vanity top.

Kash took her gently by one arm. "Come and sit down. I'll order something from room service. A stiff glass of milk, or whatever an Iowa minister's daughter claims to like."

Emotion brought a flush to her cheeks and made her eyes glitter. Her expression shifted with the myriad feelings passing through her. He couldn't read them, but was fascinated. Looking down at her with increasing appreciation, he caught his breath. And for the first time since he'd met her—had it only been earlier that day?—he couldn't ignore the desire that coursed through him, tightening him even now.

Suddenly he realized that she was searching his eyes, probably trying to find out about *his* emotions. "You really didn't have anything to do with this?" she asked grimly. "I mean, what would be the point of stealing my toothbrush? Or cartoons and old photos?"

"Perhaps you're less ordinary than you think. But no, I didn't rob you."

"Exactly what *were* you planning to do to me, then? Or rather, what *are* you planning? What happened to your big, bad threat from this afternoon?"

He studied her in exasperation, but kept a cool mask

on his face. "I assure you, if you cause me or my client any trouble, you'll regret it."

"Would you do something worse than this, or use a *different* kind of torture and intimidation?" Sarcasm cut through her voice.

"Really, Ms. Brown, we villains prefer to keep our strategy to ourselves."

"What could be worse than this? Being beaten up? Sold into slavery? Forced to eat liver and onions? I really *hate* liver and onions."

"You don't seem too worried about my intentions."

"I'm not certain why you're playing Sir Galahad, that's all."

He gestured toward his hooded eyes and tawny skin. "Sir Galahad? There's nothing English about this face."

"Exactly where are you from?"

"Virginia. I have what's known as a Tidewater southern accent. Very old and proper. Why, don't I look as if I belong among the magnolias and the peaches?"

"No, you look like you belong in a desert tent with your harem. Or in a pagoda with your concubines."

He laughed shortly, a little stunned by her perception—not the harem and concubines part, but the cultural connection. "My mother was half Egyptian and half Vietnamese. My father was an American Army adviser assigned to Saigon before the Vietnam War started. I was told that he was from New Jersey. And obviously of Italian heritage, with a name like Santelli."

Her eyes widened with surprise. Whether she approved of his mixed heritage or not, he couldn't tell. "You never knew him?" she asked.

"No." The reasons behind that weren't something he cared to discuss. He'd already told her more than he revealed to most people. Worse, he couldn't believe that he'd so easily confided personal information to her, a woman he hardly knew.

He closed his hand around her upper arm and tried not to be distracted by the firm, sleek feel of it under his shirtsleeve. "Why are we standing here chatting like two accountants who've just met at a singles bar? You've been robbed of everything you own. You should be weeping and tearing your hair out—something I, as a typical villain, could sneer at."

"There's nothing typical about *you*. If I'm not hysterical, it's because I'm not the hysterical type. I tend to become stubborn and make dumb jokes when life gets rotten. And when I've got a decision to make."

"What is that?"

"I'm going to call the Bangkok police and report everything that's happened to me today. Then I'll call the American embassy. Your name will figure prominently in everything I say."

"I love compliments."

"Don't count on them, bub."

He motioned toward the other room. "Can we sit down and hold a *civilized* argument?" He glanced around. "I never conduct important discussions in boudoirs smelling of cinnamon bath soap. Very interesting, though. Do you think of yourself as a cinnamon bun, a cookie, or a steaming cup of hot, spiced cider?"

She stiffened and gave him a fierce look. "A cold vanilla milkshake with poison in it. Please, take a big sip."

"Invitations were made to be accepted."

He pulled her to him and kissed her lightly. Her sharp gasp broke against his mouth. He held her in a loose embrace, one she could easily pull away from, but instead of shoving him away, she twisted her mouth tightly on his, then reached up and pinched his right ear so hard that tears came to his eyes. But he stood absolutely still, refusing to break the kiss, astonished at his impulse and her reaction.

He felt her tremble against him. Slowly her hand dropped to his shoulder and clenched his soft cotton undershirt. Her mouth was as mobile as his own, and just as aggressive. Waves of desire shot through him, stunning him. He was far from being a stranger to desire, but not this scalding, elemental sense of losing himself in her. When he opened his lips, she made a bitter sound of distress but parted her lips for the urgent sweep of his tongue. As she sagged against him, Kash felt his knees weaken with the power of intense, jumbled needs, aching and neglected emotions that wanted to fight their way to the surface.

Rebecca couldn't believe she was willingly holding him, that her fear and anger had been reduced to a blinding curiosity about the passion behind his dark eyes. His body was a hard wall and yet amazingly fluid, inviting hers to bend into the taut curve of his belly, the deep swell of his chest.

She quivered helplessly when his hands slid up her arms and unfurled along the sides of her neck. Tendrils of fire radiated from his fingertips as he brought his palms forward, brushing the center of her throat. Slowly he angled his hands behind her head, sinking his fingers into her hair and tilting her head up, so her mouth met more deeply with his.

Dragging her hands over his shoulders, she kneaded the hard muscles and felt them flex in response. He was the shadowy force she'd been drawn to all her life; the faceless erotic visitor in her nighttime dreams; the first man who'd ever caused her to forget everything but the primitive need for fulfillment. Her body wanted to curl around his, and every impulse urged her to strain toward him in slow, rhythmic motion.

He broke the kiss at the same moment that she wrenched her head back. She stared up at him in white-faced disbelief, breathing heavily. He realized that he must look the same way to her. He was holding her shoulders, keeping her away, and she had the same defensive grip on his shoulders.

"I want you to be all the good and decent things you claim you are," he said huskily. "I swear that nothing would please me more."

She drew shaky breaths, inhaling his musky, masculine scent. "And I wish you had enough faith in human nature to believe I'm not lying about who I am and what I came to Thailand for."

"You and I have only one choice. We can study each other and try to learn the truth."

"Study each other?" she echoed, frowning. "Don't mince words. You intend to investigate me, grill me for information, and try to catch me in lies. What were you trying to learn when you kissed me?"

Regret and anger warred inside Kash. "Just now—the intimacy—it wasn't planned. In fact, it wasn't even wise. Congratulations, Ms. Brown, you provoke me in ways no other woman has been capable of. I can't say I've ever been pinched during a passionate embrace—not on the ear, at least."

Her expression darkened. In a voice that vibrated she said, "I don't know how we ended up doing that, but we're not ever going to do it again."

"I started it, but you were trying to prove something. Are you satisfied?"

"Satisfied that you're trying to complicate a situation that's already confused beyond hope. I've been kissed before, Santelli, and I'm not a kid. I wanted you to know that."

"I think you put too high a premium on kissing. It takes a lot more to prove anything to me. Besides, I already assumed you'd been kissed before. In fact, at your age I hope you've done considerably better than that."

"At my age?" Her mouth formed an *Oh!* of dismay. She swallowed hard and shook her head in disgust. "Is everyone over the age of consent supposed to have a collection of notches on their bedposts?"

Kash arched his brows in mock dismay. He was silently trying to believe that a twenty-six-year-old woman in the modern world—even a minister's daughter, if her story was true—had never gone to bed with a man. He cleared his throat gruffly. "Not a collection, necessarily, but at least a scratch or two."

She did a double take and blinked, appearing to grow even more upset. They were plummeting into uncharted territory at dizzying speed. "I believe in keeping my bedroom furniture in mint condition," she said, her voice rising. "It'll last longer that way."

"Or just become a dusty antique, unseen and unappreciated."

"I'll marry an antique lover, then."

"Marry someone closer to your own age. The insurance is cheaper."

She muttered darkly, and wriggled out of his grip just as he raised his hands to release her.

"What a relief," he quipped. "I thought you were going to take advantage of me."

She turned on her heels and walked rigidly into the other room. Pulling open dark russet drapes, she stood in front of the window with her hands clasped tightly behind her back. The curtains framed her against the sprawling and colorful lights of Bangkok at night, a few stories below. The Chao Phraya River was a wide black ribbon winding through the landscape, dotted with the lights of barges and small boats.

"A lovely view," said Kash, walking up behind her. *She* held his attention, not the scene outside. For all he knew, tigers could have been dancing in midair. He was watching the woman who had no right to be so vivid in his imagination. "Calming to look at, if you don't let yourself wonder what's going on beneath the surface."

Her shoulders were drawn back proudly. She turned her head toward him, presenting a strong, clean profile. The face that had seemed merely pretty at their first meeting now revealed rare energy and intelligence. "I came to Bangkok because I wanted to find my half sister," she told him. "But I also wanted to encourage something new about myself, the part of me that's tired of playing safe."

Kash moved beside her and forced himself to gaze ahead. "I don't believe that you're Mayura Vatan's half sister. But I may be willing to concede that you, at least, think it's true."

"Thanks for small favors."

"I said I *may* believe that."

"Tell me about the Vatan family's feud with these other people, the . . . the—what is their name again?"

"Nalinats. They claim Mayura agreed to marry their son. She didn't. But the Nalinats believe they've been dishonored. In Thailand, loss of face is the most terrible insult. There have been some ugly incidents."

"Against Mayura? What? Please tell me."

Caution made him brusque with her. "There's no need for you to know about that—not yet, at least."

She groaned in frustration. "But these Nalinats are probably responsible for the men who attacked me and robbed my room! Don't I deserve more information? Why do you have to be so secretive?"

"My client deserves confidential treatment. When I know you better, and I've finished checking your background, we'll talk."

"You can't confide in me, but you can kiss me—twice in one day! How well do you have to know a woman before you maul her?"

"I apologize for the first time. It was an unwise tactic, nothing more. Ah, but the second time, the second time was mutual, Ms. Brown." He cocked a black brow at her accusingly. "I was carried away."

"Someone like you doesn't kiss someone like me unless there's a reason—and it wasn't my incredible beauty, okay?"

"You give yourself too little credit. But have it your way—I only kissed you in the hope that my fantastic technique and irresistible body would lure you into admitting the truth." His voice became droll. "I was a miserable failure. Oh, woe is me."

"Good-bye, Santelli. I'll take care of myself."

"You said that before, at the brothel. It was an ignorant statement then, as well as now. What do you intend to do—ask the police to watch over you? Expect our embassy to protect you from local thugs each time you leave the hotel? You can report everything to the authorities, which won't do any good at all, or you can accept my protection."

After a speechless moment she said between gritted teeth, "Accepting protection from you would be like asking a dragon to toast my marshmallows. I'd get roasted by accident."

He bit back a laugh. Her eccentric way of looking at life delighted him. "I've warmed many a woman's marshmallows in complete safety."

"Not mine."

He dropped his teasing attitude, which was strained, at best. "You're not safe in Thailand. Regardless of what you think you have to fear from me, someone much less likable than myself is your real problem. If you insist on staying, you must be as quiet about it as possible. No police reports. No wandering about the city alone."

"You just want an excuse to keep track of me twenty-four hours a day."

"That's true. But think of this, also. I have a definite reason for keeping you safe. Anyone who hurts you may well have designs on my client. So consider yourself part of your so-called half sister's security plan."

"Take me to meet her."

Kash shook his head, and felt regret. Rebecca Brown looked so wistful, suddenly. "That's out of the question."

"Why? I'm harmless! A harmless cartoonist from Iowa! I grew up in a small town with a kindly, overprotective Methodist minister for a father! I have a house with a front-porch swing and flower beds in the front yard! I'm disgustingly *wholesome*!"

"That remains to be seen." He recalled the smooth, sweet heat of her mouth, and knew that she was far from harmless, at least to him. "This discussion is closed. Accept my assistance, please. I'll provide you with a loan to replace your clothes and personal items. I'll also arrange a new passport and traveler's checks. You and I will get to know each other. Perhaps you'll come to trust me."

She was seething, her fists clenched by her sides, her whole body rigid. "Perhaps you'll trust *me*, and I'll finally meet Mayura. What you're saying is I have to do what you want or there's no chance I'll see my half sister."

"Exactly. Sorry."

She dragged her answer out unhappily. "I suppose I accept, then."

"Good." He walked toward the door, passing the neatly made queen-size bed while a surge of loneliness mingled with pure arousal. Even Rebecca Brown's anger was enticing. But only time would ease the awkwardness and resentment between them.

"One of my men will be outside your room all night," he said over his shoulder.

"Making certain I don't leave?" she called hotly.

"Making certain no one tries to harm you. But if you leave, yes, he'll go with you. By the way, I'll arrange for a few hundred dollars to be sent up to you. Pocket money."

"You have a larger pocket than I do," she said.

"I want my captive cartoonist to know how generous I am."

"Exactly what do you expect me to do while I'm under your protection? Under your protection," she repeated in a resentful tone. "That's a nicer way of saying 'under your thumb.'"

"I only want a chance to get to know you. I'm not such a cynical judge of people, despite what you think. But I *am* cautious." Kash nodded to her, and said with droll formality, "May I call you by your first name, Ms. Brown?"

"It'd be ridiculous not to, since you and I seem to be stuck together like Siamese twins."

He laughed sharply. "With a tendency to be joined at the lips."

Rebecca shook her head. "No more of that. If that's what you expect as part of this arrangement—"

"Don't." The word was spoken low and fierce, a sound like leather snapping. His eyes glittered with rebuke. "Don't accuse me of that kind of manipulation. And don't portray yourself as some sort of helpless maiden. If I ever kiss you again, you'll be an eager partner. Just as you were tonight."

She looked at him somberly, then nodded. "You didn't deserve that accusation," she admitted. "I apologize."

"Good enough. I admire your honesty."

"You don't admire it enough, or you'd take me to see my half sister."

He groaned in exasperation. "Good night, Rebecca."

"Good riddance, Kashadlin."

"Please, call me by the name all my trapped victims use. Kash."

"Kash. Gee, I feel as if I really know you now. It makes my heart all warm and fuzzy. Like a tarantula."

"You have a wonderful way with words, Rebecca. Have you ever thought of having the acid level on your tongue checked?"

"I express myself through my cartoons."

"Ah, a poison-pen cartoonist. I see."

Kash started toward the door again, but halted by a heavy, upholstered chair, where he spied a slip of paper peeking out from underneath. He knelt on one knee to retrieve it. Rebecca ran over excitedly. "They missed something! Thank goodness! I don't care what it is, I'm glad to have it!"

Kash straightened, while she leaned close to him and peered over his shoulder. The paper was folded. He opened it and studied the malevolent dragon sitting on its haunches with its tail curled over one shoulder. *Kashadlin Santelli* was written underneath in big, looping script.

"Oh, darn," Rebecca said softly. "I'm sorry."

"Considering the day's circumstances, I understand."

"Darn, I'm sorry," she repeated solemnly, sighing. "I forgot to add the horns."

Kash feigned an icy look but had to fight a smile. Even though the dragon was evil and buffoonish, it had been drawn with great skill and detail. At least he knew he'd won her attention. "Such a labor of love," he said dryly.

"I wanted to capture the real you," she muttered.

He folded the paper carefully. "May I keep it?"

"Go ahead. I'm sure I'll be drawing more. It helps me work out my feelings toward you."

"A series of personal portraits. I can hardly wait to see how I develop."

He opened the door and stepped out, then pivoted to say good night. For a long moment they looked at each other, sharing the day's intensity, the night's underlying sensuality, and for the time being, the promise of future meetings that would probably be as unpredictable as this one. "Eat well, sleep well, and rest," he instructed. "I'll be back in the morning."

"Be still, my heart," she said flatly.

Less than half an hour later Rebecca heard a knock at her door. Warily she went to it, tightly wrapped in a thick white robe the hotel maid had brought. "It is Kovit, miss," a tentative bass voice said politely.

She grimaced. Her bodyguard, courtesy of Kashadlin Santelli. Santelli's spy. She opened the door and peered out. Kovit handed her a package neatly wrapped in delicate gold paper. "From Mr. Santelli," he explained.

She thanked him, locked the door again, and went to her bed. When she unwrapped the package, she smiled darkly. He'd sent her drawing pads and pencils. And a note, written in sweeping black script as commanding as it was elegant. Her fingers played across the note repeatedly. *Dragons can be dangerous or friendly,* it said. *Depending on your point of view.*

Four

"Good morning, Rebecca. Dreaming about dragons? Here I am, back to breathe fire on your upstanding Iowa marshmallows."

Kash's smoky voice whispered against her good ear. The effect was so erotic, he might have been in bed with her. Startled, Rebecca squinted in the darkness and tried to wake up. She held the phone from the night-stand against her ear, and his voice was definitely coming from the receiver, but she glanced around the room just to be certain she was alone. A tingle ran up her spine.

"Where are you?" she croaked, rubbing a hand over her eyes, then reaching for the light. Her hand paused, then dropped back to the warm sheets. The fantasy of imagining him behind her in the darkness, leaning over her, his lips almost brushing her ear, was blatantly tantalizing. She didn't want to ruin it, she admitted.

"I've left my cave and come back to the hotel. I'm in the lobby. Where are you?"

"In bed, asleep."

"You talk very clearly in your sleep, then."

She finally got her wits together enough to notice the clock. "It's only six!"

"I'll be up in five minutes. We have a lot to do. A lot to learn about each other, isn't that right?"

"Umm, the first thing you should know is that the last time I willingly got out of bed this early, I was having my diapers changed."

"Well, if you insist, I'll bring the talcum powder and—"

"Don't expect me to speak or walk normally for hours."

"This is somehow different from last night?"

"Santelli, it's not nice to make fun of a person who's still asleep."

"You're probably smiling. It seems to me that your natural inclination is to smile often and for no apparent reason."

She frowned at the easy way he found her strings and pulled them. "Try it sometime. You might learn something nice about the world."

"I'll settle for learning more about you."

"Just more, not something nice? I am a nice person, Girl Scout material, honest, kind, brave, and trustworthy. I swear. My half sister will like me. So introduce us, hmmm?"

"It's only one minute after six, and she's already starting," he said ruefully. To her he ordered, "Turn in that merit badge for patience."

"I bet you were never a Scout."

"Noooh," he agreed, with a grim edge to his voice. "Not even close. I was busy stealing, fighting, and trying to stay alive."

She made a soft, startled sound. Before she could think of anything to say, he added brusquely, "Put a robe over your cookies, Miss Scout. I'm on my way upstairs."

Rebecca felt a little stunned as she hung up the phone. A second later she was staggering around, remembering that she'd sent her skirt and blouse to be laundered, that she had no hairbrush, makeup, toothbrush, or a gun to threaten Kash with for arriving so early and putting her in this addled condition.

When she opened the door to him, she looked up stoically into his freshly shaved face, then down slowly at his handsome chest, covered in a soft blue pullover. Cream-colored trousers encased his long legs, ending at soft gray walking shoes. Today he was as sporty as any tourist, but with this exotic, self-composed tower of masculinity, *sporty* was a panther wearing a house cat's collar. Her heart hammered in her throat. Under the curling black lashes his dark eyes examined her intently, and the look on his face was more serious than she'd expected.

"I couldn't comb my hair," she mumbled, gesturing vaguely. She hugged her robe tighter over her bare chest. "I have no clothes. I have underwear, but that's all, except for the robe, of course. I sent my clothes out."

She felt each nerve ending come alive at the thought that the glance he flicked down her body meant he was thinking what she thought he was thinking.

"I hate to spoil this enticing view, but I brought you something to wear," he said finally. His tone was neutral, but she knew he must be joking. The only enticing view at the moment was *him*, and he probably realized that she was captivated by the sight. He lifted an expensive and new-looking leather tote. "For you. Inside is an outfit for you to wear while we shop for more. And a hairbrush. And various other items I assumed most women would want. Oh, and a bottle of perfume. A cinnamon fragrance. I hope it makes you feel secure and, hmmm, *homey*." He said the last word as if it were foreign to him, and slightly suspect.

Rebecca shot him a rebuking look. "You still think of me as a silly cinnamon bun?"

"Now, now, I wasn't trying to insult you last night. I happen to like perfumes that make me think of eating." He scanned her flushed face and arched a brow mischievously. "You really want to smile. I think you would if you weren't convinced I'm making fun of you."

"You are."

"But not in the way you think. I've never met anyone like you before. Not anyone from Iowa, not anyone so *gosh-darned* cheerful. I enjoy ruffling your corn silk. But as I said last night, I like you just the way you are."

"That's not quite what you said. You hinted that I'd better not be lying about who I am."

"Because you're so different from me. I appreciate that."

Puzzled but breathless, she took the handsome tote from him and bustled away, her knees weak. "You went to a lot of trouble for this. Thank you."

"I'll be waiting in the lobby. Oh, here's your coffee." Kovit appeared with a tray. He bowed and stepped past her, put the tray on a table near the door, then glided back out. "Kovit will escort you downstairs. I have some phone calls to make."

"I'll see you downstairs," she agreed, searching his expression for clues to the man behind it. She saw a smooth tightening, a retreat, and a certain deepening of his own scrutiny of her. A trill of alarm but also burning curiosity rose inside her. What kind of man was he? How deep were his secrets?

He nodded slowly, his eyes never leaving hers. "It's going to be a long day."

After he left, she shut the door weakly, then let out a slow, troubled sigh. Kash was the most organized man she'd ever met, probably her exact opposite in that regard. *And in many other ways*, she added regretfully. She had very little reason to like or trust him, but she was falling under his spell.

After all, when he wasn't badgering her, he was doing thoughtful little things such as remembering her favorite fragrance and— Good heavens, had he gone shopping for this bag full of items in the middle of the night? Where? Didn't he sleep? She hadn't gotten more than two hours sleep herself, and if she weren't supercharged on adrenaline and Santelli's electric effect on her senses, she'd be a zombie.

She had dreamed about the mystery man who'd become her . . . her what? she asked. Her ally? Her guard? Her fantasy? Wandering to the coffee tray, she fumbled with the insulated pot, poured a cupful of the black liquid, then distractedly dunked a spoonful of brown sugar into it. She finished by squeezing a thin slice of orange into the coffee.

Kash Santelli. The Asian-Italian sheik from Virginia, with a melodic southern accent, impeccable clothes, obvious education, sophistication, and money, but she guessed that none of those fine things had been part of his childhood. He liked early mornings and carried a gun. Brothels disgusted him but were familiar territory. He made black threats and sexual innuendos but treated her with care. Without half trying, he made her feel incredibly desirable, but also naive.

"I'll go crazy if I don't find out everything about you, Dragon," she said out loud. "You're not the only one who's smart enough to pry out important details."

Feeling determined and strong, she took a sip of coffee. With a soft gasp she set it down and stared at it. Orange slices. Brown sugar. How had he known she liked them? Somehow, while she'd slept, he'd researched her and learned the quirky way she fixed her coffee. What kind of man had the means and determination to find out so much about her?

She slumped down in a chair and looked at the cup as if it were her most intimate secret, and Kash had just served it to her with a deadly, warning smile.

The morning had gone quietly—too quietly, Kash thought, as they drank frothy Thai iced tea inside a tiny streetside café. Only the sounds of conversation around them, the click of chopsticks on ceramic bowls of spicy noodles, and the soft whir of ceiling fans filled the silence between them. He watched her eat delicately, trying with obvious determination to conquer her chopsticks and the noodles, and also trying to ignore him as much as possible, which she'd done all morning.

She'd come down to the hotel lobby in a subdued mood, and hadn't said much to him over breakfast or in the hours since, as she shopped for clothes to replace her stolen ones. Kovit lumbered along behind them, as curious and intrigued as a chaperon, so maybe she'd felt awkward or shy. But Kovit had been sent back to the hotel with her purchases.

At first Kash told himself that her withdrawn attitude was a blessing; he needed the quiet time to observe her and silently sort out his emotions. No other woman had ever made him feel this way. He alternated between exhilaration and confusion.

Her moodiness began to grate on him. Where was the stubborn teasing, the humor, the fascinating storm of emotion and conversation he'd expected? He was churning inside because she wouldn't speak to him. He, who rarely craved more than his own thoughts, much less a near stranger's conversation, was an emotional mess because of this troublesome woman, a stranger who might have hidden intentions toward the client he'd pledged to protect.

Kash pushed his lunch aside and frowned at Rebecca as she ate. *Talk to me,* he ordered mentally.

"Smart monkey," she said, her gaze riveted to the tiny, agile animal that was peeling fruit for its owner, a street peddler, under an awning just outside the café. "I wonder if it knows that I like to squeeze an orange slice into my coffee?"

A quick flood of understanding made Kash tilt his head and look at her pensively. "Ah-ha. You had your darkest vice exposed, and you're feeling threatened."

"No more than usual, since I met you."

She switched her cool gaze to him with the directness he'd craved all morning. The blue of her eyes was even more vibrant, accented by the blue-and-gold silk dress he'd given her at her room. The traditional Thai skirt wrapped around her snugly and reached her midcalf, and the matching top fit closely and was nipped in at the waist, with short, capped sleeves and a stand-up collar. When she swung her head a certain way, her brunette hair caught at the gold piping along the collar's edge. He fought a constant desire to reach over and caress the different textures. The smooth skin of her throat invited his touch, as well.

"I'm not accustomed to having someone investigate me behind my back," she said scornfully. "I guess I expected you to investigate me face to face, listen to what I had to say about myself and my background, and see for yourself that I'm telling the truth."

"Look at it this way. Through the miracle of modern communication, since yesterday I've acquired an extensive file on you from my researchers in America. They've confirmed all the basic facts. You're twenty-six years old, have a degree in commercial art, sold your first cartoon in high school, lived with your father until you were twenty-three, teach Methodist Sunday school, own a small, neat house in a small, neat town, and make approximately thirty thousand dollars a year selling a cartoon strip about life in small-town America." He paused to take a sip of his tea.

She watched him wide-eyed, her mouth open. "Go on."

"According to newspaper articles in your hometown paper, you're widely regarded as odd but likable, and the only scandal in your life occurred last year, when you broke your engagement to the mayor's eldest son, one Leonard 'Leon' Cranshaw, who had been your steady since junior year in high school, where he was voted 'Most Likely to Wear White Dress Shoes and Plaid Jackets.' I'm very curious about Leon."

"He was a nice guy, with clean fingernails and no imagination. I don't appreciate you bringing him into this. Or checking up on me at all."

Kash raised his hands in supplication. Secretly he

was pleased. She'd showed good taste in ridding herself of Leon. "You weren't meant to have a safe, boring relationship with a man."

"Thank you, Mr. Manners, for the advice."

"I'm sorry my investigation makes you angry. But consider this—now I don't have to wonder if you're really who and what you say you are." He spread his hands magnanimously. "I've put us light-years ahead in getting to know each other."

"Oh? Will you give me all the details of *your* life, so we'll be even?"

He nodded, then leaned forward and propped his chin on one hand. "I'm thirty years old, I have a business degree from Harvard, I work for my adopted father's private security service, I'm unmarried, honest, honorable, but not the most lighthearted person in the world. I'm a firm believer in not believing. If anyone hurts my loved ones, they hurt me. If I'm assigned to do a job, I finish it. I know how to fight. There. You know me."

"Thanks for the detailed info. I'll write it down on the back of a stamp."

"I've told you what you want to hear. It's the truth. If I told you more, you wouldn't like it. I'd never fit in with your warm little vision of the world."

She chuckled fiendishly. "I've already made up much worse stories about you than could ever be true. So talk."

Kash shook his head slowly, and watched the taunt fade from her eyes. He had the disturbing notion that she sensed the darkness in him, and he wondered if she was afraid of him. The thought that someone like her would be shocked or disgusted by his childhood didn't surprise him. He'd been careful over the years never to discuss his past with anyone, after a few pitying and repulsed people had hurt him with their reactions.

"You can't imagine," he said grimly. "But never fear, the dragon won't breathe fire on your angel wings."

She brought her chopsticks up in the air as if she

wanted to reach across the table and pinch him. "So now that you've used some kind of sleazy private-eye team to check on me, am I innocent? Does it matter that I'm exactly what I said I am?"

"It helps. And by the way, the organization I work for—my father's organization—is one of the most respected private intelligence groups in the world. We take only high-level cases. In fact, this minor job for the Vatan family is only a favor. My father was an old friend of Mayura's uncle. Ordinarily we specialize in international terrorism and kidnapping cases."

She looked suspicious but intrigued. "You must make a lot of money."

"At times. But I was adopted into a wealthy man's home, so neither he nor I do this work for the money. My father is interested in giving something beneficial back to society. And we do."

"Why should I believe that, when you won't believe *me*?"

"I have no reason to deceive you. No personal involvement with the Vatan family. Nothing to gain."

"So you say. But you think I could be lying about my reasons for wanting to meet Mayura?"

"Exactly. It's my job to be suspicious."

"No, I think it comes naturally to you." She made a growling sound of disgust, dropped her chopsticks on the table, and rose abruptly. Snagging the small white purse she'd bought to match the white flats she wore, she slung the long strap over her shoulder, gave Kash a menacing look, and walked away.

He tossed some bills on the table and went after her, sliding his hand around her bare forearm as he caught up with her on the crowded sidewalk. The contact brought them both to an abrupt, highly charged stop. "Be patient, Corn Blossom," he said as lightly as he could. "We're making progress."

"You're making progress," she retorted, "but I'm getting a royal Siamese pain."

"Let's walk and enjoy the scenery. A block or two from here we can stroll along one of the prettier canals."

"I don't 'stroll' in this elastic bandage of a skirt, I wiggle."

"Yes," he admitted, giving her a sideways glance. "Every inch of you. That's the scenery I was referring to."

A flush crept up her cheeks, but she squinted at him defiantly. "Since you've found out everything about me, you must know that I've never worn anything provocative in my whole life. So why'd you buy this dress for me—as a joke?"

Kash dropped the taunting attitude and looked at her with a troubled frown. "Take a chance. Be who you want to be. I suspect you want a dress like this, that you're dying to be admired for something a little more exciting than your good manners."

"Nothing in a research file could have told you that."

"No," he agreed. His fingers ached to stroke the satiny skin of her arm. "Sometimes a man just goes by instinct. And hands-on experience. Judging by what my instincts tell me, I predict you'll be completely corrupted by the time I'm done with you. You won't know your wiggle from your walk."

"That can work both ways, Santelli. I'll have you so turned upside down that you won't be able to find your cynical attitude from a hole in the ground. You'll be ready to join the PTA and sing in the church choir."

Kash gave her a tightly controlled smile. She chortled. "You're worried," she proclaimed victoriously. "You're actually worried."

Feeling undone, he pushed her firmly along the sidewalk. "Wiggle," he growled. Her accuracy and continuing laughter, a soft, pleased snicker, pestered him, making him want to tell her how ill-suited he was for her fantasy. Everything he'd survived and all the years of adjustment afterward had turned him into a loner, guarded about his emotions, bewildered by the family life he saw all around him. He thought even Audubon, who had tried very hard to help him adjust, never expected him to fit in.

"Why so quiet, Dragon?" she asked slyly several minutes later, when they were threading their way along a canal dock crammed with Thai shoppers and lined with peddlers.

"I'm enjoying a daydream." He nodded toward the murky water. "What a colorful splash you'd make."

She turned to scowl at him, but his attention was already taken by three Thai men who were idly browsing through a vendor's silver trinkets. Alarm raced through his blood. Casually he took Rebecca's arm. "Don't turn around and stare at them, and don't appear shocked. But we may have an unwanted audience."

Her face paled. "Who?"

"Three men over by the silversmith's cart. They were outside the restaurant when we left. It's just odd that they'd end up here too."

She didn't flinch. His admiration for her steady nerves translated to his hand's reassuring squeeze on her arm. "Do you think the Nalinat family is after me?" she asked.

"I think they're convinced you know where Mayura is. If they can find her, they'll try to force a marriage between her and their son."

"Is that legal in Thailand?"

"In this part of the world family relations and saving face are more important than the law."

"But I can't tell them anything. Couldn't we just explain to the Nalinat family that I'm an outsider to this whole feud?"

"They'd never believe it."

She trembled against his hand, though her face remained calm. "I'm not some kind of spy for them, I swear it. Even if you never believe my story about Mayura being my half sister, even if you always suspect my motives for coming here to meet her, don't ever turn me over to the Nalinats."

The desperation in her voice sent a white-hot surge of protectiveness through Kash, even though such fierce gallantry made him feel a little foolish. The world wasn't made of heroes, only human beings trying to save what little hope and happiness they could. "What, you'd rather stay with me?" he asked in a gruffly teasing tone. "You find me preferable to a family of scheming, cold-blooded Nalinats?"

Her mouth crooked up at one corner. "Only a little."

"Good. Then come on. We'll make sure those apes over there can't follow us."

He grabbed her hand and led her down a set of weathered wooden steps to the edge of the canal. It was packed with long, flat boats, each guided by peddlers who squatted in the rear under small canopies, with their wares spread out in the hull for people on the street to see. Merchants would maneuver to the docks for shoppers to reach them. Farther out, bigger boats with cylindrical coverings were home to entire families and their merchandise. To Rebecca, the big boats resembled floating Quonset huts.

"Step carefully and follow me," Kash instructed her. Then, to an old man seated in one of the small boats crowded up to the dock, he said in Thai that even Rebecca could understand, "Excuse us, please."

The next thing she knew, Kash was tugging her aboard the narrow vessel, and she was trying very hard not to step on ripe fruits piled to overflowing. "Don't bounce. Step from boat to boat," he told her. His strong, confident grip pulled her along firmly as she cringed and tiptoed from one teetering surface to another, her breath frozen in her throat.

"Excuse us, please," Kash said repeatedly, smiling broadly and bowing to each merchant they passed. His smile was a glorious flash of white, a marvel of incredible charm. "The only time you show your teeth is when you want something," she accused, casting her gaze down hurriedly as she almost stepped on a black duck.

"You smile for your needs, I'll smile for mine," he called over his shoulder. "Mine are practical."

"So are mine. Smiling reminds me that the world is basically a happy place. Ow! A crab reached out of a crate and pinched my ankle!"

"Smile at him. And don't tell him he's going to be someone's dinner tonight. He might not agree with you that the world is so happy."

"Cynic."

They finally landed on the box-filled deck of a large boat. Kash pulled her behind him through an open flap in the curved canvas hut. A wide-eyed family of five looked up from a meal. Rebecca stared back at them in mutual discovery. Kash dropped her hand, then pressed both of his in a low, respectable *wai*, smiling again, as if he and she had just dropped by to visit old friends.

Rebecca listened in bewilderment as he spoke to them in fluent Thai, motioning to her and then himself. The family's patriarch lost his wary look. His brows shot up with excitement. He and Kash exchanged a long series of hand gestures and words, dramatic grimaces, and shaking of heads. Finally Kash sighed and nodded. Suddenly the whole family was smiling and making *wais* at both of them.

Kash glanced over his shoulder at her. "We've made a deal. They've sold me their boat."

"This one?"

"No, a smaller one. I'm in no position to press my luck. I'm giving them a ridiculous amount of money as it is. And all the extras."

"Extras?" she echoed warily.

"Our clothes. They're poor people, and these clothes are worth a lot to them."

After a stunned moment she said under her breath, smiling at the family to be polite, "Not *my* clothes, bub."

"They'll trade. You won't be naked. The point is for us to disappear into the crowd of boat merchants. We'll head upriver, away from the market. I'm tried of strangers following us. I want a chance to talk to you, not spend my time wondering if we're going to be jumped from behind."

He pulled a handful of local currency from a sleek black wallet and paid the man. The others gathered around with stunned expressions on their faces. Rebecca assessed the family's matriarch. She was all of five feet tall. Rebecca was five-eight. She tapped Kash's shoulder tentatively. "In case you haven't noticed, this lady is about half my size."

"She says she has clothes to fit you. Have pity on me, for godsake. Her husband is trading me a piece of cloth for *my* clothes. No more arguing. I want to get out into the canal."

The family bustled about, the children giggling and watching Rebecca with graceful almond-shaped eyes, while she and Kash waited under the curved ceiling, amid blankets, small chairs, a camp stove, and small crates packed neatly with the family's possessions. "Pardon me, do you work in this department?" she asked Kash dryly. "Could you tell me where the changing rooms are?"

His worried eyes flickered with amusement and mischief for an instant. "We're in it. Coed. If you dare peek at me, I'll blush."

"I doubt it."

"Do I look like the kind of man who's used to undressing in front of women I hardly know?"

"*Yes.* Including my half sister, who I imagine you know *very* well."

Surprise flooded his expression. "Is that what you think?"

"Why shouldn't I?"

"No, I don't know her that well, and no, she's not your half sister."

They were interrupted by the wife, who placed a bundle of clothes in Rebecca's hands. Rebecca smiled and nodded at her, while darting a worried look at the pale cotton trousers and thin, short-sleeved shirt. Both were well made and clean, but much too small.

The husband brought a square of thin white cloth to Kash. Then the whole family bowed out of their floating hut and dropped a canvas curtain over the entrance. Dim light coming through an air vent in the ceiling enveloped Rebecca and Kash. She looked at him blankly, clutching her bargain outfit to her middle. They were packed in the tiny space, only an arm's reach from each other. "We can't even go to opposite sides of the room. I guess we can turn our backs."

Kash chuckled fiendishly, unable to resist provoking her. Blood pounded low in his belly at the thought of their intimate circumstance, but he had too much on his mind to relish it. Her belligerent stance and accusing air brought out the rebel in him. "Go ahead and turn around," he instructed. "Then I'll be able to ogle your cinnamon buns without being obvious."

"Good," she said dryly. "Glad you're not being inconvenienced." With a huff of exasperation she pivoted, dropped her new clothes on a crate, and fumbled with a button at the back of her collar. Her pulse was pounding, and not just from the anxiety of being followed by the suspicious men on the dock.

The boat rocked slowly, a sensual sway, and the only sounds in the dim, close interior were the soft rustle of material being unbuttoned and opened. She flung a quick look over one shoulder and saw his bare back towering only inches away. His lean, muscular-looking rump, still covered in the handsome cream trousers, was so close, she warned herself to be careful bending over.

Slowly she pulled her silk blouse over her head and laid the rich, flowing colors aside. Unexpected tears stung her eyes. *I don't want to give up this fantasy dress*, she admitted wistfully. When she finished putting on and buttoning the plain cotton shirt, she felt as if she'd been stuffed into a gauze glove. The buttons strained over her breasts, and if she twisted just so, the shirt gaped open. She could see the rosette of lace at the center of her white bra.

The metallic swish of Kash's zipper sent a corresponding zip up her spine. Her skin tingling with curiosity, she gritted her teeth and pushed her long silk skirt down her legs. Something solid and flexing and just about the size of his rump rubbed against her pantie-covered hips, as in a smooth, hard caress. She jumped, then turned to look warily at him.

"Sorry," he said without much sincerity, as he bent from the waist to pull his trousers and shoes off his feet. With a slow intake of breath Rebecca scrutinized his nearly naked body, big and supple, clad only in snug black briefs—regulars, not the bikini type, darn it.

His rear was thrust out, almost brushing her body with each slight movement he made. It was a sleek curve of power and angular masculine shapes, the most perfect enticement a woman could hope for, and Rebecca swallowed harshly as reckless urges captured her hand, making it want to reach out and tweak him just to feel the combination of smooth black cotton and hard muscle. And to prove she could take his dare.

"Better not," he said glibly, and suddenly she realized he was watching her from under the taut, sinewy line of his arm. "I'd have to reciprocate. It'd only be fair."

"I only wanted to see where you store your ego."

"I'll turn around, then."

"No, I've had all the laughs I can stand in one day."

"A lesser man would shrivel at such mean words. I assure you, Corn Babe, I haven't shriveled an inch." His dark eyes fluttered coyly. It was such an absurd and calculated gesture from a man so unfrivolous and stern that a laugh burst from her throat. "I thought we were in a hurry."

"You're the one who stopped to ogle the first male behind you've ever seen close up."

"And you're the one who's using this opportunity to look at my legs."

"Forgive me, but I haven't seen legs that long since an ostrich ran across my sleeping bag in Africa."

"All right, all right, long and skinny and pale, I know. I've heard the jokes since I was old enough to walk. But they're my legs, and I like them."

"I only said they're long. That's all I said. You obviously haven't shown them to the world in a few years, because they don't look the way you think. They must have evolved."

"I walk a lot. Miles."

"Great muscles. And white panties. I'm not surprised."

"This has gotten out of hand," she said darkly, tugging the tail of her shirt down over most of her behind. She turned away from him again. "I'm sorry I ever started this discussion."

He managed to plant his fanny against hers again as he finished removing his shoes. "My, my, I can't control it," he uttered, deadpan. She edged away from him and jerked her faded beige pants up her legs. The pants fit like the shirt—tightly on each curve. The hems stopped in the neighborhood of her upper calves. The center seam had the effect she'd always imagined a thong bathing suit would produce. Rebecca squirmed and tried to stretch the material, but had little success. She frowned down at herself and said ruefully, "I've been preshrunk."

Kash straightened, and she felt soft, cool cloth brush against her hand. They turned to face each other at the same time. She coughed and studied him with disbelief. "It's a diaper," she said.

"It's a very practical way of wrapping a cloth around yourself and between your legs," he countered. "Very comfortable."

He pushed the waist down an inch so that it hung low on his flat, muscle-streaked belly, nuzzled by the curly black hair that swirled inward beneath his navel. With the center of the white cloth tied up loosely between his legs, the material hung around his thighs in graceful swoops, exposing the fronts in teasing glimpses of muscle and skin.

Rebecca had long since stopped analyzing his physical appeal. It was simply something she had to stay far away from, like a tornado posed at the edge of her safe boundaries. But appreciation careened through her senses.

"Nice outfit," she realized he was saying to her. His gaze traveled down the thin cotton. "Good wiggling potential."

The Thai woman pulled the canvas flap aside and looked in. Rebecca carried her silk skirt and blouse over. The woman's eyes lit up, and she grasped the material happily, but soon frowned and peered at Rebecca's chest, while saying stern and disappointed sounding words to Kash.

He cleared his throat, but the strangled humor was still evident. "She expects your brassiere, as well. Off with the goods, Ms. Brown. We've wasted too much time already."

Rebecca gazed hard into the woman's eyes, found no hint of retreat there, and sighed heavily. She stalked back to her former spot, turned her back, stripped off the shirt and bra, then put the shirt back on quickly and buttoned it. At least it didn't gape open over her breasts anymore. It didn't have to. Her alert nipples were already straining against the tight cotton.

She presented her bra to the woman with a curt *wai*. To Kash, she said dryly, "I believe I'll survive. Let's go."

His arched brow belied the nonchalant once-over he'd given her new look. "Your wish is my command, O perky one," he said, and bowed.

She threatened to hit him.

Five

A few minutes later they had settled under the small canvas awning of a boat not much larger than a canoe, with a puttering little outboard motor. Rebecca sat in the front, watching Kash steer from the back, his long, handsome legs stretched out on a bamboo mat on the bottom, his bare feet casually crossed at the ankles, his chest and abdomen gleaming with perspiration, his usually stylish black hair ruffled by the hot breeze. The hint of the Orient in his features combined with his comfortable attitude to make an enchanting picture. Even as thoroughly Western as he was, he belonged here, too, framed by the panorama of Bangkok— brilliantly colored Buddhist temples, palm trees, tiny huts on stilts wading in the canal's edges, boats filled with Thai families.

Transfixed, Rebecca peered at him from under a straw hat with a flat top and broad brim. The hat looked like a squashed volcano, and she suspected it gave her a laughable appearance. But suddenly she felt at home, despite being stuffed into tight pants and a shirt that screamed the feminine details of her body, despite being worried about the men who'd been following them, despite the upside-down turn her life had taken in the past two days, and the mysteries of the man who lounged across from her now, watching her watch him.

"I knew it," Kash said sardonically, but his gaze stunned her with its stark appreciation. "You found something to smile about. What?"

"Adventure. I love it."

They motored up the canal for a long time in silence, and each time her eyes were drawn to him—which was often—she found his meeting them, warm and intrigued, as if he'd momentarily called a truce and only wanted to enjoy the sight of her. Serenity was an unexpected companion in their aimless, slow journey. She trailed one hand in the dark water, curled her bare toes and studied the interesting curve of them on the bamboo floor mat, and told herself she was one dumb Iowa bunny for feeling so joyful about being with him. Even telling that to her common sense didn't make her enjoy him any less.

"Where are we going?" she asked finally.

"There's a public garden at the canal's edge, a little farther up. We'll stop there. We can walk to the nearest street and take a taxi."

"You've been in this kind of situation before. You seem to know exactly what to do."

He shrugged lightly. "It's my work."

"Can your work be dangerous?"

"Sometimes."

"Do you travel a lot?"

"Yes. Most of the time."

"What made you take the assignment to protect Mayura Vatan?"

"I speak Thai and know this part of the world so well. My father and I agreed that I was the best choice."

"How many people work for your father?"

"Several dozen. They're a close-knit group. They treat each other like family."

"You sound as if you're not part of the group. Why?"

"Only because I'm a loner at heart. I'm used to being on my own."

"You aren't close to your father?"

"In all the important ways, yes. But I was eight years old when he adopted me. And I came from an unusual background. I was never able to make the adjustment completely. I prefer to go my own way."

"Your background?" she said in a leading tone, and waited for him to fill in the rest.

"The garden." He nodded toward an apron of perfect lawn and graceful Thai statuary that fanned out to a strip of pearl-white pebbles beside white stone steps descending into the water.

"Your background," she repeated.

"Your nipples," he countered.

She craned her good ear toward him. "I beg your pardon?"

"Your nipples. They're beautiful." Rebecca's mouth popped open. He gave her a predatory smile. "Conversation over."

A few minutes later they were sitting on the lawn with a shield of bright red flowering shrubs behind them and the canal in front. The mottled walls of a magnificent old home lined the opposite shore. Atop were stone creatures having women's heads and bodies and cats' hind legs. Their hands were pressed into reverent positions beneath their chins, and their ornate costumes exposed their thrusting breasts. The sweeping, feminine curves of their bellies descended to triangles of a much darker stone. A brooding fantasy villa of peaked roofs and towering trees loomed above the wall.

"I don't know who lives there, but he's got a strange notion of what women look like," Rebecca said giddily. Her head whirled from lack of sleep and the emotional strain of the past two weeks, but mostly from Kash's disturbing effect.

"Are you all right?" he asked, placing a hand on her shoulder. The contact seared her through the thin shirt, and waves of sensation crested in the sensitive peaks of her breasts, making them as hard as those of the stone women-cats.

She wondered if he noticed. Undoubtedly. Santelli was the kind of man who noticed everything about his prey. But his voice was so smooth, so deep and luscious. It lulled her strained, tired mind. "I'm exhausted and confused," she murmured, rubbing her forehead. Slowly his hand moved down her back, his fingertips stroking rivulets of pleasure over each vertebra.

"Lie back on the grass. Rest. I'll make sure no one bothers us."

"What is this?" She blinked owlishly at him, her eyes heavy with fatigue. "A trick? A tactic?"

"I believe it's called a nap." He clucked his tongue at her reproachfully.

"Hah. I think I hear a dragon purring. Probably means something bad's about to happen."

"It's possible that we can trust each other, you know." He hesitated, searching for words, then said gruffly, "I believe your story about why you came to Thailand. Even if you're mistaken about being Mayura's half sister."

"That's the best news I've heard in a while." Rebecca looked at him with tears in her eyes, and a crucial part of her caution dissolved into the warm, fragrant afternoon. "I really want you to believe me. I know the story about my father being Mayura's father sounds unlikely, but he had no reason to make it up. Neither do I."

His dark gaze was as fluid and caressing as the canal's flowing water. "So you traveled all the way here because of your father's story, because you respected his word so much."

She nodded. "He was the kindest, most decent man in the world. I wish my mother hadn't died when I was a baby. I've heard they were a wonderful team."

"What an unusual life you've had," he said pensively.

"Unusual? No. The most ordinary life in the world. Nothing exciting ever happened to me."

"How marvelous that sounds. You don't know how lucky you are."

"Kash? You don't like to talk about your own life very much, do you?"

"No. It's not important."

"Of course it's important. It's *you*."

"No, I've worked very hard to make certain it's *not* me, and I don't think you'd like the details."

"Try me."

His gaze bored into her. She almost swayed, hypnotized and bewildered by the myriad emotions there—the guardedness, the anger, but also a shadowed urgency, as if he was trying to understand her and gauge her reaction to what he might say. "Rest," he said finally, and looked away. The shutter had come down on his thoughts, once again.

"I played a cloud in a third-grade class play," she told him. "And I was supposed to dance with a boy cloud. But we kept bumping our cardboard costumes together. That's the way I feel with you right now."

"I'm sure you made a pretty thunderhead."

"No, I couldn't hear on one side because my hearing aid fell out. I stepped on the boy cloud's feet. He kicked me in the shins. We weren't exactly Astaire and Rogers."

"Your poor ear," Kash said softly. He reached up and pushed her hair back a little, then stroked a finger across the hearing aid and the tender earlobe beneath.

She inhaled raggedly. "I lost most of the hearing in my right ear when I was five. I caught an infection from swimming at a pond. Every other kid in the neighborhood swam there, but I was the only one who got sick. That's sort of the way my whole life has gone. I'm blessed with being different. Sometimes it's good—it's what made me a cartoonist—but sometimes it's bad."

Rebecca frowned. "But you probably know all that. It

must have been in the research your people did on me."
She said the last sentence grimly.

He gave her an apologetic look that melted her anger.
"I know that you've been partially deaf in one ear since
you were a child, but I don't know how it affected your
life. It must have been hard to adjust. Tell me."

Rebecca cleared her throat and looked away. "My
father wouldn't let me do anything risky after that. I was
overprotected. Drawing helped me fantasize. That's why
I became a cartoonist. My cartoon alter egos can do
everything I can't."

Sighing, she lay down on her side and pillowed her
head on her arms. Now she found herself gazing
straight at his taut back, as he sat beside her with his
legs drawn up. His shoulders flared into strong arms
marked with ridges of veins and muscle. Low on his
spine the muscles met in a shallow valley just above the
carelessly wrapped cloth covering. She envisioned
pressing her palm to that fantastic terrain and sliding
her fingers up his backbone, then down, down, until
finally they were under the cloth.

Kash twisted to study her. She raised startled eyes to
his. In that electric second she suspected he could read
each one of her thoughts. Abruptly he reached over and
trailed the backs of his fingers across her cheek, then
unfurled them and slid his hand behind her head.
Drawing her up a bit, he leaned down to meet her
mouth with his own.

Surprise and arousal surged through Rebecca's
blood. Sleepiness was banished; every nerve in her body
scalded her with sensation. Her hands rose to his
shoulders, then flattened and slid around him. In that
flash of agreement they were in each other's arms,
holding tightly and kissing in wild, abandoned exploration. Why him? Why? her mind cried desperately. Why
did this man, who wouldn't offer her any of the traditional values she'd been raised to love, cause her to lose

control after twenty-six years of dedicated self-restraint?

But the frenzied passion of their kisses banished her thoughts and made her hold him even tighter. She explored his back while moaning into the hot caress of his extremely skilled mouth. Rebecca wanted his hands on her body, wanted to feel his lips on her breasts, needed to have him deep in her aching center, filling her, explaining the mysteries she'd always imagined.

He gently slid a hand under the tail of her shirt. With his warm fingers stroking magic into the small of her back, she quivered and felt him quivering in return. That he could be so affected by her awed Rebecca and made her reach for his head, where she petted the smooth, straight hair in gratitude and eagerness.

His caresses were unhurried and intoxicating as he drew his palm around to her stomach. Shivers of desire ran down her belly, and she could barely breathe. The shirt buttons strained over her breasts, and the friction excited her skin. Lost in speechless wonder, she continued to kiss him deeply, until his hand slid upward and gently closed around one of her swollen breasts. With a low moan of pleasure she broke away from his mouth and looked up at him in a daze. His own eyes were half-shut but glowing with reassurance, while his expression was savage with passion and control. The combination excited her even more. As he slowly circled the tip of her breast with his thumb, she quivered and lifted her mouth to his again. A throaty, encouraging sound rumbled in his throat. She thought she'd die with joy.

"You can trust me," he whispered against her mouth. "Trust me with anything you want, anything you need, anything you want to talk about."

Anything you want to confess, he meant. The mood shattered like fine crystal. Rebecca jerked her head back and stared up into his brooding eyes. "You want me to talk. That's why you're doing this."

He exhaled roughly, looking troubled. "I want you, period. As for the rest—I mean it. Yes, I want you to talk. If you've got something to hide, tell me. Because I *don't* want it to come between us anymore. I want this relationship to become much more personal, and it can't do that until the other problem is cleared up."

"Much more personal? Isn't that going against your style? And aren't you busy enough already?" Sheer frustration and disappointment brought tears from her eyes. "Are you and my half sister having an affair?"

"What the hell— Where does that keep coming from?"

"If you use sex in your work with me, you must use it with other women too. You must use every tactic that makes your job easier. Because that's what you're obviously doing with me." She pushed his hands away.

"I don't—I am *not* sleeping with my client. And when I say that I want you, I mean it in a purely personal way."

"And if I don't spill my terrible hidden secrets to you, would you still want me? *No.* You'll find some other way to keep me with you until you can convince me to go home. Is that what all this is about—distracting me until I get tired and leave? I have to know. Maybe this doesn't mean anything to you, but it means a lot to me. Why are you trying to make me fall in love with you?"

The word *love* was like a slap. He froze. Deep surprise showed in his eyes as they searched hers. Rebecca gave a silent moan of despair and understanding. Of course she didn't mean anything to him. And by being straightforward enough to mention love in connection with lust, she'd complicated their already difficult relationship.

"You shouldn't be surprised to learn that I take these things seriously," she said in a pensive voice. "I won't apologize for that. I know it seems unsophisticated to you, but to me it only seems right to think about who I want to love, and why."

"There's no love between you and me, and there never will be," he said, his voice whiplash sharp. You'd have to know all about me and accept everything about me, just as I'd have to know you. It won't happen."

His bitter words stunned her. Any romantic fantasies she'd had about him dissolved in his stony glare. "You're in no danger," she said finally. Answering him without giving away her humiliation took tremendous effort. "I wasn't thinking straight when I used the word. That was the problem—I forgot how much I need and expect from a man. It won't happen again."

That only made him look fiercer. But his voice was deadly calm as he said, "I've been trying to understand why you affect me so much. I should have been reminding myself that a woman with your background judges every man as a potential husband."

Completely shaken now, she answered through gritted teeth, "If I were desperate for a husband, I'd be married by now. Don't insult me by thinking you're a candidate. You seem to be pretty oversensitive on the subject. I'm sorry for the ugly things that happened to make you that way, whatever they were. I'm sorry, but I don't deserve your bitterness. The world is *not* as bad as you think, and the best traditions in *any* culture are built on family and home life, not on misfits like you."

"And you," he countered.

"Yes. But at least I know what I want, and I'll find it someday. I want a home, a mate who's my partner and friend as well as my lover, and children who know they're cherished. All the things you find unnecessary."

"And overrated."

"I wish you'd known my father. You'd see where I learned my values, and how sincere they are."

"Your father practiced what he preached?"

"Yes."

"You're certain?"

"Absolutely. There wasn't a more idealistic man in the world."

"He stood for truth, honor, and apple pie."

"Yes. Don't make it sound silly."

"It's not silly. There are many ways to uphold your ideals. I have mine, believe it or not. And I'm honest about them."

"So am I. And so was my father."

"Really? It's time for a reality check." Kash pulled her upright and, holding her by the forearms, turned her to face the ominous villa across the canal. "Look at that place. It doesn't mean anything to you, does it?"

"No! Why should it?" As his intentions sank in, she struggled against his grip. "You know something about it that I don't know! You brought me here deliberately! You don't ever do anything without a purpose, do you?"

He held her tighter against his hot, bare chest. "Take a good look at it. A very wealthy Thai man lives there. A retired art smuggler and gambler. In his younger years he was the most notorious thief in Bangkok." Kash paused for effect. "And he was a close friend of your father."

Rebecca gasped harshly. "It couldn't be. That's not the kind of man my father would have liked."

"Your father was a guest at that villa many times while he was stationed in Thailand with the army. He visited often with the thief and the four beautiful young women who lived—and slept—with the thief. I want you to understand that *your father didn't tell you the truth about his years in Thailand.*"

She dug her fingers into Kash's hard arms, which were now around her waist. "Maybe it doesn't mean anything. There must be an explanation. Have you talked to this man? Is that what *he* told you about my father?"

"*Yes.*" Kash bent his head close to her good ear. His breath blew swift and rough against her neck. His lips brushed her ear with mocking charm. "He said your father helped him smuggle stolen Thai art objects to the States."

"No!"

"And that he never married anyone, much less had a child."

"My father wasn't a criminal, and he *was* married to Mayura's mother!"

"He must have been an incompetent smuggler, if he went home to America and become a small-town minister to make a living."

"My father was incapable of stealing," she said in a taut, gritty voice. A fireball of disbelief and anxiety shot through her blood. "Someone lied about him." Nearly strangling on emotion, she added recklessly, "I can prove it."

"How?" Kash twisted her around to face him. Defensive, she braced her hands on his chest, though touching the seductive wall of firm muscle and satiny black hair made her want to cry for the tenderness they had shared only moments before. His expression was a shrewd mask, with an underlying urgency that looked almost like pain. His conflicting feelings made her despair of ever understanding him. "How can you prove it?" he asked fiercely.

"We have to go back to the hotel." Rebecca became icily calm. "I'll show you. I don't feel like explaining right now. I want you to see my evidence, first. We're not doing too well with trusting each other's word, so why pretend that we ever can?"

His dark eyes seared her with their troubled, intense gaze. Then resignation settled in them, and he looked exhausted. "Trust has very little to do with what's between you and me," he agreed, nodding slightly, an elegant but somehow tragic gesture. "And it would have only led to a different kind of trouble. Maybe it already has."

Without another word he set her away from him and got to his feet. He held out a hand, but she ignored it, wearily pushing herself up, then walking ahead of him, her head high. A tight knot of gloom sat in her chest. "If you don't want trouble, don't ever touch me again," she said over one shoulder.

In an instant he caught her, pulled her backward against him, and placed a hard, lingering kiss on the side of her neck. She whirled around and slapped him, even as he was releasing her. They stared at each other across a sizzling span of anger and amazement. "Don't make threats you can't keep," he said, but seemed more upset than stern.

"Don't make promises you can't keep," she replied.

Kash had never felt so emotionally drained. Standing in Rebecca's room, waiting for her to open the small felt bag she'd gotten from the hotel safe, he hardly cared about the mysterious proof of her father's story. He kept thinking of the bitter words he'd spoken to her when she'd mentioned *love* as if she expected to fall in love with him, as if a woman like her could. He kept remembering the shattered look in her eyes as she'd listened to him cut the idea to shreds.

To be loved by someone like her was a fantasy he'd never allowed himself to consider. The kind of love she meant—the lifetime commitment, the bonding, the sharing that went beyond sex and companionship to a merging of innermost dreams—seemed impossible for him. His furious reaction had come from the pain of self-denial and brutal experience.

Kash scowled as he watched her untie the delicate strings that held the bag shut. Her hands were smooth and strong, callused on the right thumb and forefinger from what he assumed were countless hours spent gripping paintbrushes and drawing pens. The nails were short and pearly clean at the tips, with a coat of clear polish. Even dressed in the revealing cotton pants and shirt, with her bare feet grimy and her hair a disheveled, mink-brown jumble, she had an air of nourishing niceness.

"I have a piece of jewelry that belonged to Mayura's mother," Rebecca said in a dull voice. "I had two pieces—a necklace and an earring—but those men at the brothel stole the necklace."

Kash willed his haunting thoughts away. "Your father gave them to you?"

"Yes. They were gifts to Mayura's mother, and after she died, he kept them. But one of the earrings was taken when the Vatans stole the baby. They took as many of her dead mother's personal belongings as they could find."

She slid the earring onto her palm and watched it shimmer in the light of the lamp on the dresser. It had three dangling pieces of sterling, the tiniest no longer than a pea, the largest as big as a penny. Each was inset with an oval of jade, and around the jade was intricate engraving.

When she placed the earring in Kash's hand, he looked closely and saw endless swirls of flowers, so tiny that only the most skilled hand could have etched them.

"Turn it over," Rebecca said wearily. "Read the back."

The largest section was engraved in English with letters so small Kash had to squint to read. *To my beautiful wife, Nuan.* Mayura's mother. And there was a date: 1960.

"Not long before he died, my father gave me that and told me the other earring says 'From your loving husband, Michael.'

Kash closed his hand around the delicate piece of jewelry. "Why didn't you show this to me before?"

"I was hoping to save it for my meeting with Mayura." She looked despondent. "It was something very personal, something I hoped she'd recognize."

"After over thirty years, do you really expect to find the mate to this? It was probably lost when Mayura's mother died."

Rebecca raised startled eyes to his. "Do you mean you believe it's real? You believe me?"

"I believe you, but not your father. I'm sorry."

She turned away, her shoulders sagging, and hugged herself. "What now?" she asked in a voice hoarse with defeat.

"I'll show this to the Vatans and listen to their comments."

"They'll only say it's a fraud."

"Do you know any reason why your father would make up the story he told you?" Kash asked gruffly. He was tired of hurting her. Her pain radiated through him.

She pivoted and met his gaze with a cold, rebuking stare. "The story is true," she said flatly. "The Vatans are the ones who've made up a lie. Please take the earring and leave."

Kash hesitated, wanting badly to say something to soften her despair, but knowing that his words—and actions—had done nothing but give her the wrong impression of him since they'd met. Or was it the right one? Unsentimental, suspicious, a loner—he was all of those. He was also much more vulnerable than she thought, but only the people who knew him best recognized it. Sometimes when she looked at him with glowing approval in her eyes, he hoped she sensed it.

"Kovit or one of the other men who work for me will be on guard outside, if you need anything or want to go anywhere," he told her. "I'll be back as soon as I can."

"Just phone me," she replied calmly. "I really don't care to see you again."

He nodded, while disappointment warred with grim reality. *She's trouble*, he reminded himself. "You're right. That's for the best."

He left her standing in the middle of the room, looking as miserable as he felt.

"I thought you'd come here," he said behind her.

She jumped at the grim, deep baritone with its aristocratic Dixie lilt. Rebecca pivoted swiftly and looked up into Kash's shadowed face. He stepped into the flickering gas light of a slender street lamp. It cast charcoal and silver streaks through his black hair.

Rebecca's heart felt like a butterfly inside her chest. "You *let* me get away from Kovit. I should have known. You wanted to follow me and see where I'd go."

"No. Kovit called me frantically and said you'd tricked him and left the hotel. I thought this was the most likely place you'd go."

He cast a glance at the tall stone wall with its mysterious women/cat sentries and ornate iron gate. Inside was a courtyard, and beyond it, looking very traditional and exotic, was the thief's home. "I know you wouldn't be happy until you asked him yourself about his friendship with your father."

"You're a mind reader," she said bitterly. Rebecca studied him in morose silence. Casual white trousers and a simple white pullover met at his belted waist. The buckle, she noticed with distraction, was of woven gold, similar to the slender watch on his left wrist. On his feet were smooth white shoes, almost like slippers. His appearance was graceful and streamlined, but very masculine. His broad shoulders and muscular arms were a striking contrast to his lean, lithe build. She'd never seen such a unique combination of vivid physical power and the trim refinement of a ballet dancer.

His dark gaze had returned to her too. He scanned the simple blue silk jumpsuit she wore with gold sandals. His anger was evident. "Did you think you could leave the hotel unnoticed? Good Lord, after what you've been through, weren't you afraid someone other than me would follow you?"

"I had to take the chance."

"If you'd been picked up by strangers again and hurt or killed, I'd have—"

"Been rid of me for good, and happy about it," she finished sharply. "Don't lecture me about my safety."

The quick tightening of his face accented his unusual

features. Suddenly she'd never been more aware of the hawkish nose and deep-set, alert eyes, the savage thrust of his lips. "You're the one who'd like to run from temptations," he told her, speaking very softly, like satin pulling across steel. "I can control mine."

"Bully them, you mean."

"You need bullying. Otherwise your foolishness might ruin you. Come with me. There's a car waiting for us just around the corner."

He swept a hand toward the handsome road, with its sprawling, perfect homes and mantle of trees. Across it and beyond the thief's villa, a dozen yards away, a side street peeked from behind someone's courtyard wall.

"You sat there in a car and just waited for me to arrive," she said angrily, tears of frustration burning her eyes.

"While my men were searching everywhere else for you. I'm efficient."

"And I'm stubborn. I'm not going back to the hotel with you."

"We're not going to the hotel. Your things will be packed and brought to you. You come with me."

She stared at him in disbelief. "I'm through doing what you tell me to do."

Before she could pull back, he took one of her clenched hands and wound his fingers through hers tightly. "We're not through with each other at all." There was nothing gentle about his grip.

"What's changed, then?"

"You've been invited to stay at the estate of Mayura's aunt." When she gasped softly, he nodded and gave her a slight bow. "I admire your persistence. The earring intrigued her. She wants you to be her guest. She wants to learn more about you.

"Where will you be?"

His eyes burned into hers with their mocking unhappiness. "With you. She's afraid of barbaric foreigners, you see. I'm to instruct you in civilized behavior." She yelped with insult and continued to look at him in astonishment, even as he began tugging her along beside him, to the car.

"You, instruct *me*?" she said sardonically. "*I'm* not civilized?"

He turned to her in the middle of the dark street, framed by the night, taking her breath away with the unsettling look he gave her. "You will be," he promised smoothly. "When I get through with you."

Six

In the moonlight the estate of Mayura's aunt rose out of the forest in splendor, a collection of peaked roofs with gracefully upturned eaves, like a Thai dancer with her fingers upswept. Kash drove their car through high stone gates, along a winding drive bordered by lawns and trees, into a courtyard dominated by a shrine in the center, surrounded by colorful flower beds.

Kash ushered her inside a bright, modern hall that took her breath away. Under bent ebony lamps that cast angular shadows, ornate teak furniture vied for her attention along with luxurious rugs, ceramics, jade statuary, and vibrant wall hangings.

"Am I really welcome here?" she asked.

He made a soft, deep sound of sharp amusement. The pure male confidence of it annoyed her, but made a heated pool in her belly. "Let's just say that you're an intriguing nuisance. Madame Piathip wants to observe you up close."

"That makes me sound like a strange new species of wildlife."

"Wild? I'll have to find out how wild you can be."

"I'm as tame as a hamster, by your standards."

"I've never known a hamster who could cause so

much trouble." Kash guided her by her elbow, his grip possessive and controlling, as they followed a smiling, elderly manservant up a long marble staircase. "Piathip Vatan is a little eccentric," Kash told her. "Just give her your trademark smile and don't say too much."

The tiny, white-haired woman sat among gorgeous silk pillows on a curved lounge with elephant heads carved into the armrests. Her doll-like body was swathed in miles of pink-and-gold silk robes, but her hair was done in a short, elegant Western style, and her makeup was as chic as a model's. Rubies glittered at her ears and throat. Her dark eyes burned from a lined but youthful face. Behind her were arched windows that looked out into the tops of magnificent trees, and underneath her feet was a large Oriental tapestry rug.

Rebecca listened to the sound of her pulse throbbing against her hearing aid as she and Kash crossed Madame Piathip's chambers. Both of them made respectful *wais* to her. Rebecca felt the searing scrutiny of her narrowed gaze.

"You're so large and pale!" Madame Piathip exclaimed. "How can you possibly think you belong to my family?"

Rebecca stared at her in surprise. "I only want to meet my half sister. I don't mean to intrude on the Vatan family."

"Mayura couldn't be your half sister. It's impossible. Why, there's no resemblance at all!"

"I don't think that means anything," Rebecca said as politely as she could.

"It's certainly ridiculous, your story. Mayura's father was a British Army officer. My sister married him when she was eighteen years old. He was killed in a military accident not long after she died."

"She died in a private hospital in Ayutthaya, of hepatitis," Rebecca said calmly, nodding. "When Mayura was one year old."

Madame Piathip's eyebrows shot up. "How do you know these things?"

"My father told me. He was with her when she died."

"He was quite nosy, quite! How dare he investigate a stranger's sad circumstances."

"He was her husband," Rebecca said between gritted teeth. "I wish the family would acknowledge that. I don't understand why you won't. I can't imagine what you want to hide."

Madame Piathip gasped dramatically. Rebecca thought of a Siamese cat that had just been goosed. "She's truly rude and uncivilized!" Madame said to Kash. "You promised to instruct her!"

"I apologize," Kash answered smoothly, and Rebecca swore she heard amusement in his voice. "I haven't had much time with her yet. She doesn't mean to be rude. Forgive her. She's a foreigner."

Rebecca swallowed harshly and met Madame's wide-eyed gaze with a neutral one, though she burned with exasperation inside. Madame said primly, "Mr. Santelli says you're sincere and harmless. I only invited you here to correct your confusion. I'm sure you'll see that you and Mayura couldn't possibly be related. You'll see that her world is very different from yours. We'll be patient with you, so you can learn."

Rebecca chewed her tongue, then nodded stiffly. "Thank you, Madame Piathip, for your consideration."

"You see, Madame?" Kash interjected quaintly. "Her manners are already improving."

Rebecca held her temper until they were downstairs, following another servant through a maze of short hallways filled with delicate furnishings, bamboo rugs, and tropical plants. "I guess it would be impolite for me to strangle you."

"Patience, barbarian. You're in Thailand now. Be peaceful and open-minded."

The servant showed them to a large, carved door set in an alcove with white stone walls. Inside was a beautiful little bedroom done in rich silks and teak furniture. A lovely bed piled in pale, shimmering covers and pillows sat beneath a high, arched window. Outside, the feathery limbs of a tree brushed the window's stone sill. Her belongings from the hotel were neatly stacked on a table. Through a door in one corner was a modern bath with luxurious scarlet linens and gold wall lamps.

Kash stood behind her in silence. She felt his eyes on her as she wandered around, touching the dark, sleek furniture and rich fabrics. When she turned to him, feeling flushed and aroused for reasons she couldn't define, he said softly, "This room might corrupt you before I do."

"As long as you're not here to 'instruct' me, I'm sure I'll be able to resist."

That comment didn't sound the way she'd meant it. He smiled wickedly at her obvious dismay. "Good night. I'll be in a room just around the corner. If you need anything."

"I'll order out for a pizza, thank you."

"There are dozens of servants, and most of them speak English. They'll bring you whatever you want." His eyes flickered coyly. "As soon as you admit what it is."

"Hmmm. That reminds me, I have a gift for you."

She rummaged through her things and found her drawing paper. Rebecca handed him a carefully folded sheet. Giving her a somber look, he opened it and studied the coiled, cruelly smiling dragon. The dragon's bulbous behind was covered with a baggy piece of cloth fitted like the one Kash had tied around himself.

Kash said drolly, "This isn't accurate. My teeth are more pointed."

"I'll capture the real you eventually."

"The 'real me' is beyond your reach."

"I have a long reach."

"And a vivid imagination."

"It's working overtime, trying to figure you out."

He went to the door, his expression troubled, his chin

raised in the intractable but somehow appealing way she was coming to recognize. His eyes met hers in a challenge that made her knees weak. "In the Orient, mysteries are best left unsolved," he warned.

After a breakfast of fruit and rice they walked outside into the lemony morning sun and strolled side by side down a pebbled garden path. It led away from the sprawling house among magnificent trees and flowers, all as neatly arranged as the landscape of a bonsai dish. Rebecca clasped her hands behind her back. The dappled light caressed her bare shoulders above a modest but formfitting white sundress. The appreciative look Kash had given her when she stepped out of her bedroom made her vividly aware of her body. Even the faint stirring of a flower-scented breeze made her skin tingle.

Kash's arm brushed hers as they walked, and she darted glances at him. His white pullover and pleated white slacks gave him a breezy tropical attitude, especially in combination with his black hair and golden skin. She felt his presence in her blood like the warm breeze, stroking her from the inside out.

"You said you were only eight when you left Vietnam to live in America," she said, searching for casual conversation. "And that you come back to this part of the world often."

"Yes."

"Then you must have had at least few good memories from your childhood."

"The people and their customs will always be a part of me."

Rebecca sighed. She suspected that vague answers were the best she'd get. "How many languages do you speak?"

"I speak Vietnamese and Thai fluently, and I can manage fairly well in Chinese."

"I love Chinese script. Can you write Chinese?"

"A little."

They entered a glade by a small brook. Rebecca inhaled softly in wonder over the stone bridge across it and the perfect lawn under a drooping willow. Even the rounded stones at the water's edge seemed to have been artfully set there. "Everything has its place, and there's such harmony in the arrangement," she said breathlessly. "That's at the heart of Eastern philosophies, isn't it?"

"Yes. There's serenity in knowing your place and fitting in well."

"Do you have serenity, then?"

He laughed darkly. "I admire it. I understand it. That's a start."

She sat down on the smooth cushion of grass and tucked her feet under her. Kash dropped to his haunches beside her. When she glanced at him, he was watching her. "You have serenity," he said. His eyes searched hers as if he could find the reason and absorb it.

"I don't think so. I want so much."

"What?"

"A combination of wild excitement and cozy routine. Adventure and safety." She smiled. "Dorothy loved the land of Oz, but she was glad to get back to Kansas. I'm like Dorothy, except I want to take Oz home with me." The intensity in his eyes made her look away and pretend to study a blade of grass. Rebecca smiled pensively. "How do you write 'greedy' in Chinese?"

He sat down close to her, picked up a twig, then took her hand and held it palm up. Slowly he drew invisible Chinese symbols in her palm. Trickles of sensation slid through her blood. Without thinking she dipped her head closer to his, watching the twig move across her skin, feeling every fiber of her body react to his hand cupping hers. Warmth flooded her cheeks and made the breeze feel fiery on her lips.

"That says 'greedy'?" she whispered.

His eyes met hers with dark, almost feverish, attention. "It's more of an abstract idea. 'Eager to be pleased' is what I wrote."

She was hypnotized. "That sounds better."

"There's no harm in wanting to be pleased, Rebecca. Sharing pleasure doesn't mean you've given up your ideals. It's not selfish. It's human. You're a vital, passionate woman, and you shouldn't ignore what the world offers you."

"What am I being offered?" she asked, her tone full of meaning. They looked at each other for a long moment, unanswered questions churning in the silence.

"Just . . . pleasure," he whispered. "Pure and simple. As innocent as it is uncomplicated. With no hidden motives, no games, no manipulation. And you control it. You let the pleasure serve you, and when you want to stop, it will stop."

Her breath shattered in her throat. "That sounds too easy."

He raised a hand and stroked a fingertip along her lower lip. "Thais believe in moderation, not self-denial."

"This is one of the lessons you intend to teach me?"

He nodded. "If you're willing to learn. Open your mind. Relax. Trust your instincts as well as your self-control."

"I've never been less certain of either."

"I disagree. You know *exactly* what you'd like to do at this moment. Take a chance. Indulge yourself a little. Trust yourself. Trust *me*."

With a broken cry of confusion she kissed him. His muffled growl of encouragement exploded in her senses just as his welcoming caresses drew her into his arms. He lay back on the grass with her beside him. Still kissing with infinite care, they slowly stroked each other's faces and hair.

Rebecca was stunned by his tenderness. It was even more profound than before, unhurried, exquisitely tuned to her sighs and the smallest shiftings of her body. She braced herself on one elbow and leaned over him. His chest was a broad, enticing hardness under her sensitive breasts.

She drew a hand down his shirtfront, mesmerized by the swift rise and fall of his stomach, tingling at the thought that he was hers to enjoy, but afraid of the reckless urges rising inside her like a tornado. "Your touch is the most exciting thing I've ever felt in my life," he told her. "Just feeling your fingers on my face makes me fall apart. Don't stop."

Shattering emotion curled around her. His strength attracted her, but his gentleness won her. It always had. She could no longer doubt that under the layers of defense was a man with needs as fragile as her own. The kisses they shared held wonder and hope. She caressed his jaw with the backs of her fingers, and he sighed happily against her parted lips. This man couldn't hurt her, it was beyond him to do that. She knew it in her soul.

His hands were stroking small ecstasies on her bare shoulders. They slid down her back, tracing the zipper of the sundress's snug bodice, trailing down to the swell of her hips, then back up, with luxurious light caresses, then harder, deliciously rough ones. Her legs tangled in his, and suddenly he rolled her onto her back. She drew him down to her for one devastating kiss after another, and his arms went under her in a tight, possessive embrace.

Rebecca's senses were swimming with desire and the blinding knowledge that she would never meet another man who tormented her with wild passion but made her feel safe at the same time. "I do trust you. I do," she said raggedly, stroking his sides with trembling hands. "And I want to know more about you. Whatever you can share." She hesitated for a fraction of a second, then added in a low, emotional voice, "If it's easiest for you to share your body first, then I'll start with that."

She kissed him but felt stillness sliding through him.

He held her tightly and kissed her back, twisting his mouth on hers as if he couldn't get enough of her. He pulled his head back, his breath warm and coming fast on her lips. Surprise and a troubled frown shadowed his face. "Touch me," he said gruffly.

He took one of her hands and guided it to his stomach. Her heart pounding, she stroked the shirt for a few seconds, then her hand drifted down to the edge of his trousers. Her eyes remained riveted to his as her hand moved lower. When it settled lightly on the thick ridge, the flash of reaction in his half-shut eyes and the quiver that ran through his body made her kiss him suddenly. A small, fervent moan sounded in the back of her throat.

But at the same time he gripped her forearms and carefully pushed her from under him. His frown had become a distracted, almost bittersweet expression. He sat up. His shoulders were hunched with tension, and the sculpted muscles of his back flexed harshly under his shirt as he took deep breaths. Propping his arms on drawn-up knees, he put his head in his hands and rubbed his face wearily. "I can't do it," he said. His voice was hoarse and angry.

Rebecca clutched a hand over her stomach and sat up also. Watching him desperately, she felt a cold weight form under her breastbone. "Do what?" she whispered.

"Take advantage of your enthusiasm."

After a few speechless attempts to make sense of what was happening, she finally gave up and placed a hand on his shoulder. "I don't understand. I thought something had changed between us. I thought you wanted me to do this."

"I do. I don't." He groaned, a fierce sound that was so painful, tears of shock came to her eyes. He twisted to look at her. "I want you to make love to me but not care about me. I don't want to care about you." At her involuntary sound of grief he quickly took her hand and lifted it to his mouth. He kissed it hard. "But I do care about you, and that's why this isn't going to go any further. I want to walk away from this job without looking back. I want to walk away from *you* without looking back."

"How can you turn off your emotions that way?" She got to her knees and knotted her hands in her lap, clenching them into fists of confusion and anguish. "Why isn't there any possibility that you and I could be happy together?"

"Because your definition of happiness means having cozy little heart-to-heart conversations. I don't want to share who I am with you. I don't need to. I just need a woman who lives for the moment and doesn't ask questions."

"A woman who doesn't really care about you," Rebecca countered. "A woman who doesn't care about anything except what you can do for her in bed. I'm sure you can do a lot, and do it very well, but isn't it a little lonely to give somebody nothing but the pretty parts of yourself?"

"My parts stand on their own merits," he joked coldly.

"Kash," she said in bittersweet rebuke. She grasped his hands and leaned forward, trying to analyze the glimmer of despair in his eyes. "What are you afraid of? Don't be afraid of me."

"I'm only afraid that I won't be able to keep my hands off you, and you'll expect more from me than I can give." He rose to his feet and pulled her up with him. "Let's go back inside. I'll teach you something safe, like how to play Thai gambling games. Then I'll turn you over to Madame Piathip for the afternoon. I have business in Bangkok. I won't be back until tonight."

She slid her hands out of his grip. "You can turn your emotions off much more neatly than I can."

"I've practiced all my life."

"I feel sorry for you."

Sardonic humor appeared in the bitter line of his mouth. "You won't after I teach you to gamble. I'll win every kernel of corn you own."

She started up the path to the main grounds of the estate. Shivering with anger, she called over her shoulder, "You've already taught me to gamble. Now I'm just trying to decide whether to call your bluff."

As soon as Kash walked into the great hall late that night, the servant's nearly uncontrollable amusement told him something strange was happening. The man's enormous smile had a strained edge to it. "Madame Piathip wishes for you to visit her immediately."

Frowning, Kash followed him upstairs to the gilded doors of Madame Piathip's suite, which were cracked open. The servant popped inside while Kash waited, impatiently wondering what Madame Piathip wanted and how long it would take, because he'd hoped to stop by Rebecca's room before she went to bed.

The servant hurried back, opening the doors wide. "You may go in." His eyes were worried above a wide smile.

Kash strode into the large room and stopped abruptly. Madame Piathip sat primly on her delicate lacquered lounge, her feet crossed on silk pillows, mint-green silk robes billowing artfully around her.

Across from her, half-draped across a similar lounge, with huge pillows propping her up, Rebecca lay like a rag doll, head lolled back, arms stretched limply on the pillows around her, eyes half-shut. Her robe was pale blue, with fine embroidery at the neck and on the edges of the long sleeves. Her bare feet hung listlessly off the end of the lounge.

"Do come in," Madame chirped, folding her hands around a teacup in her lap. "I want you to take Miss Brown away. I'm through with her."

For all his attempt at control Kash nearly ran to Rebecca's side. She gazed up at him with an owlish blink, her expression serene but still alert enough to show she was upset at what had happened to her. He could see the mildly distressed look in her eyes, as though she'd had too much to drink and vaguely hated it. The blue in her eyes was eclipsed by dilated pupils, making him think of the dark eyes of a wounded deer.

"Glad to see you," she said softly, her voice slurred and yearning. She kept her eyes trained on him as if "glad" was an understatement.

Protectiveness and anger boiled up inside him as he pivoted to face Madame Piathip. He knew he couldn't voice his fury at what she'd done to Rebecca. The rules in Thai business relationships emphasized politeness to an extreme; even a mild complaint about the matriarch's tactics would have been a grave insult to their relationship. Insulting her would mean Kash's dismissal, and that would mean giving up his link to Rebecca.

So he chewed the inside of his mouth, pressed his hands together, and made a very respectful *wai* to Madame. "As one who serves your family's interests in the matter of Miss Brown, I need to know what has happened here tonight, please."

Madame Piathip nodded solemnly. "She'll be fine by morning. I just put some opium in her tea, to make her be still. Foreigners move too much. She's so large and active, she frightens me. I wanted to see what she'd say when she was quiet and serene. I thought she might tell me things."

"And did she, please?"

Madame sighed. "No. Only about Iowa and cartoons. She's very smart, for a foreigner. Would you carry her away now? I'm tired of her, but she won't leave." Looking distressed and pampered, Madame Piathip scowled at Rebecca and said in a scolding voice, "I don't think she can walk."

Kash bowed quickly. "I'll be most happy to take her away for you. Good night."

"Good night."

He bent down and lifted Rebecca into his arms. Her head drooped on his shoulder, and she managed to slide an arm around his neck. Her helplessness and the small sound of welcome she made nearly drove him out of his mind with concern for her. Physically she was all right, he felt certain, but he doubted that her straight-arrow lifestyle had prepared her emotionally for this. For the first and probably only time in her life, she was stoned.

"You're rotten and sneaky," she mumbled to Madame Piathip, then smiled drunkenly and raised one hand under her chin. After a second Kash realized it was a one-sided *wai.*

"Oh, carry her away," Madame ordered, dolefully shaking her delicate gray head.

Kash left the chambers quickly. Once he was outside in the hallway, he halted long enough to bend his head and kiss Rebecca gently on the mouth. "Don't worry. You're safe. I'll take care of you."

She smiled and met his scrutiny with glazed eyes. "I know."

Downstairs in her room the moon was sending a large rectangle of light across her bed through the deep-set window high on the wall. Kash placed her on the bed and pulled the pale silk covers out from under her. "Don't leave," she said wistfully, wobbling to a sitting position and drawing her knees up. She pillowed her head on her arms and looked at him tearfully. "I can't remember what my cartoon characters' names are. That scares me."

Kash knelt on the bed and took her face in his hands. Tilting it into the moonlight, he caught his breath at her mystical beauty, and burned with desire he couldn't indulge. "You've been drugged," he whispered. "Don't try to make sense of anything right now."

She brightened, and looked a little calmer. "That's the way it always is when I'm around you."

He chuckled, feeling better now that he had her in a private, secure place and could protect her. "See? Nothing unusual, then. Relax."

"Relaxing . . . would be unusual." She put her arms around him loosely, holding on to the back of his shirt as if that were the only way she could keep her arms from sliding off. Kash groaned silently and shook his head. "Stop." She turned her head and kissed the palm of his hand, which still cupped her face. "Thank you for being here," she murmured, her lips feathering his skin.

"I'm sorry for what happened to you tonight. I didn't know anything about Madame Piathip's silly little plan, I swear."

"Hmmm." She began nuzzling his palm, with her eyes shut. "You smell like pineapple. I love pineapple."

"Shh." He was going out of his mind. His body was begging him to caress her. "I'd rather corrupt you when you're sober."

"This isn't . . . about corruption." She frowned slightly, only her closed eyes showing above his hand, where she was now placing small kisses deep in the cup of his palm, the most sensitive spot. "It's about taking care . . . of you."

"Taking care of *me*?" he repeated with strained humor, his eyes riveted to her.

"Teaching you."

"Teaching me? What do I need to learn?"

She opened her heavy-lidded eyes and nearly destroyed his control with a look of shimmering devotion. "To let someone fall in love with you. With all of you, even those things you say no one could love."

"Go to sleep," he said brusquely, releasing her and gently pulling her arms from around him. He quickly pushed her legs down, then planted his hands on her shoulders and pressed her onto the bed. She went willingly, but reached up and began stroking his face with the backs of her fingers. His hands trembling, he smoothed the pillow under her head. "I'll be nearby all night. Go to sleep now."

"I'm not sleepy. *Kash.*" His name, spoken softly and urgently, sounded like a plea. "Just hold me. Hold me, please."

He looked down at her with strangled misery, wanting to hold her and reminding himself that there wasn't a chance in hell he'd let himself do more than that. He loathed people who took advantage of innocent sexuality, and no amount of her delicious torture would break down his control. It would be safe to lie down and put his arms around her, though. She'd be asleep in seconds. Torture for him, but worth it.

"I'll stay until you fall asleep," he promised.

She held up both arms to him with such complete trust, tenderness filled his throat. Carefully he stretched out beside her liquid body. Her robe was a swirling river of pale blue around her breasts and down her belly, pooling into shadows between her legs.

She flowed against him, her hands tucked against his chest. He cuddled her with one arm under her head and the other around her waist, and allowed himself to stroke the center of her back. Her low sigh of pleasure feathered his neck like a kiss.

Kash angled one leg over her knees and molded her to his torso, but when she tried to press too close to his thighs, he put his hand on her hip and held her still. "No fair," he murmured against her forehead, then gave into the temptation to kiss the spot.

"Yes," she whispered, and began fumbling with his shirt buttons.

"No." Kash let go of her hip and gently wound his hands around hers. She tilted her head back and kissed his chin. "Yes."

"No." He tucked his chin and looked into her dreamy eyes. They shared the same pillow, and its pale silk cover reflected a silver sheen of moonlight onto her face. "You have to go to sleep," he said gruffly.

"Why?" She wasn't being coy, she was answering from a peaceful haze that didn't care about the consequences.

"Because I can't reason with a woman who only knows 'yes,' 'no,' and 'why.'"

"Yes, yes, yes." She aimed a kiss at his mouth and missed, but caught it the next time, even as he tried to turn his head away. Her lips were warm and relaxed. Kash shivered with restraint and told himself there was no harm in a kiss—none to her, at least, because she was more playful than aroused.

He melted into her depths very softly, loving the awkward, endearing way she explored his mouth and the little sounds of pleasure that purred from the back of her throat. Lost in the taste and warmth of her, he let go of her hands and put his arms around her again.

Time pulsed slower as they continued to kiss, and the fragrant night air curled through the open window with a faint cinnamon scent that made Kash's head swim because it mingled with Rebecca's. Slowly one of her hands, light as the air, trailed down his side and came to rest on his thigh. Her fingers curled and uncurled curiously, then danced languidly down the front of his trousers.

He inhaled sharply, wishing he had all of her around him at that moment so he could move with exquisite care and show her how wonderful she made him feel, and how he could make her feel in return. His body flexed strongly with response, and he groaned silently as he pulled her hand away, then tucked it back into place between his chest and hers.

"You Iowa girls can't resist anything that reminds you of corn." He heard the raw, uneven sound of his voice.

"Touch me . . . the same way," she whispered against his lips, dragging her mouth back and forth across his.

"No, Becca, I can't. I wouldn't be able to stop, if I let myself do that."

"Becca," she echoed groggily, smiling. "Like that."

"Good, It'll be my private nickname for you."

"Kiss Becca some more." Her hands fumbled with the front of her robe, and by luck or fate, suddenly the small opal buttons were undone and the embroidered material hung open halfway to her waist. Kash drew back in surprise, then caught his breath at the sight of her breasts.

"Please," she whispered raggedly.

With a low murmur of defeat he sank down and took one of her nipples in his mouth. Her broken moan of delight made him shudder. Flicking his tongue across the swollen tip, he forced his mind away from the deep pulse of desire in his own body and concentrated on pleasuring her.

He left the straining peak with a soft kiss, then drew his mouth across her torso, taunting the delicate skin with his lips. He gave the same intimate attention to the other breast, and her soft moans cascaded into the silence, exploding in his senses. "More," she urged, writhing against him.

Kash was drowning in her magic, and the restraint he thought he'd mastered began deserting him. Breathing harshly, he dragged his head up and rested his forehead against hers. "I can't. We're going too far."

A poignant sound of protest came from her throat. "Make love to me."

Love. He took her roughly by the shoulders and pushed her away, put her on her back and knelt beside her, glaring down shakily into her wounded eyes. "You don't want to be my lover. You don't know anything about me. You don't want me. Say it. Believe it. *Say it.*"

"*No.*"

To his sorrow she began to cry, though she didn't make a sound. She struggled to push herself up on her elbows, then turned away from him. Her shoulders shook. Kash was distraught. Finally he realized that despite all they'd been through together in the past few days, he'd never seen her break down like this. Only his rejection had the power to hurt her so much.

Stunned, he put a hand on her shoulder and stroked carefully. In a low, choking voice he told her, "Don't you understand? I don't want to hurt you. I don't want to make you hate me. I don't want to come between you and all those nice little ideas you have about men and women and love."

Between harsh breaths she managed to whisper, "I've waited all my life for you."

Something broke inside him. He lay down behind her and pulled her back to his chest. *I've waited all my life for you, too,* he told her silently. But out loud he only said, "You've waited for a man who doesn't exist, who's not the way you expect a man to be."

He listed to her cry for a long time, and kept his head back from hers on the pillow, afraid that he'd give in to the urge to lean over her and smooth her tears away with his lips. By the time she quieted and began to breathe in a slow rhythm that signaled sleep, he was trembling. Hours passed before he fell asleep, feeling more alone than he ever had in his life.

The moon had disappeared, leaving the room in darkness. Kash was a large, quiet form beside her, lying on his back with his arms over his head. He was fully dressed, even down to his shoes.

After she woke up, Rebecca turned to her side and watched him sleep. Her mind was fuzzy, and her eyes felt as if sand had been rubbed across them, but she remembered everything she'd said to him, and what she'd tried to do, and how he'd responded.

What happened to make you so caring but so afraid of being loved? she asked him silently, desperately. Who hurt you when you were young?

Finally she asked herself the most important question. What could she do to break down his bewildering fortress? Every instinct cried out that the walls around him weren't as strong as he wished.

I love you, she told him silently.

Seven

He was gone when she woke up the second time. Rebecca lay in the plush bed staring pensively at the empty pillow beside her. A deep ache of bewilderment and disappointment grew in her chest, and she slowly traced the indention his head had made in the pillow.

The invisible man. It was appropriate.

Dizzy and light-headed, she sat up and put her head on her knees. Fury at Madame Piathip soared through her blood. "Sample this wonderful tea," Madame had said innocently. Rebecca remembered the fog of relaxation overtaking her mind, and Madame leaning forward eagerly to ask questions about Rebecca's father.

Looking down at the empty space beside her, she felt her throat close with embarrassment and sorrow. She'd begged Kash to make love to her, but he wouldn't. He'd been so gentle, so loving, but he wouldn't *love* her.

For the first time she wondered if she really wanted to meet Mayura. If she was a pampered, mean-spirited prima donna like her aunt, Rebecca didn't care to find out. She rubbed her head wearily, knowing even then that she couldn't give up until she'd met her half sister and tried to convince her of the truth.

Rebecca's heart twisted. She couldn't give up on her

father, either. She had to know the explanation behind his relationship with the art thief. She had to make Kash believe in him the way she did.

Kash. She sank her head in her hands. Getting through his mysterious barrier was the hardest, most painful task of all.

Rebecca tilted her head back and looked up. *I know what I want, and I want him.* She clenched her fists and cursed silently. The cursing shocked her. She didn't understand anyone here, especially not herself.

Someone knocked at her door. Walking unsteadily and scraping her hands through her disheveled hair, she went to it. Kash entered with a tray of coffee, fruit, and muffins. He wore gray shoes, pale gray trousers, and a tailored linen shirt of a rich blue-gray color. As usual, he was handsome in a way that mingled wealth with sensuality; there was an aura of command about him, in his brusque movements and the elegant nod he gave her as he walked past.

"How are you this morning?" He asked it in a conversational tone, as if he hadn't spent the night sleeping next to her, as if they hadn't shared a sizzling variety of emotions.

"Mad at the tiger lady upstairs. If I knew how to tell her off and still be polite about it, I would."

He nodded. "She's arrogant. But she's also frightened and vulnerable. Mayura is her daughter, in a sense. She couldn't have children of her own, and in a country as traditional as this, that's hard on a woman's self-esteem. According to what my father has told me about her, her husband deserted her because of it."

"To me that says she had even more reason to steal Mayura from my father."

"There's no evidence of that. She doesn't know what to make of your story. Or of you."

"You don't know what to make of me, either. You didn't even want to wake up beside me."

After he set the tray on a table near the bed, he turned

to face her. The silence between them was fraught with meaning. "I thought it best to leave while you were still asleep."

"I wouldn't have begged you for favors again." Her face burning, she wrapped the flowing blue robe around herself and sat down on a hard teak chair across the room.

"You look very uncomfortable and righteous," he said. "But beautiful." His voice was somber, and his severe expression chilled her. "Go home to Iowa. Marry a nice man. Someone who'll never disappoint you."

"You have no idea what disappoints me," she said in a low, gritty voice. "But you think you understand what's good for me. I'll tell you what I expect from a man. I expect him to have enough respect for me to let me make my own decisions. I expect him to believe in my strength and maturity. I expect him not to protect me from phantoms only *he* can see, but won't explain to me."

Kash turned from the table, as tall and unyielding as a pillar of stone, his gaze cold. "My father will arrive this afternoon. I've asked him to speak with Madame Pia-thip. Because he's known her a long time, he may be able to convince her to treat you better."

"You're ignoring everything I just said."

Striding to the door, he paused for a second and gave her a look that stopped her breath. It made her think of smoky light trapped inside a diamond. "I feel your accusations like a knife inside me," he said simply. "But I'm very good at ignoring how I feel, in order to do what's best for all concerned."

"What's best for you, you mean."

Before he walked out the door, he gave her a slight nod, as gallant and formal as a stranger's.

Rebecca waited beside Kash in a garden room filled with orchids. Audubon, who'd arrived from the airport in a private car less than an hour before, was upstairs in conference with Madame Piathip. Rebecca had been struck by his majestic appearance—a patrician but gracious face, thick silver hair, a tall, athletic body, and an impeccable black suit. Audubon had the charm and sophistication of an Old World gentleman, but there was also an air of rugged physical ability about him.

It was easy to see that Kash mirrored his adoptive father. But Audubon had a peaceful aura that Kash lacked. Rebecca liked Audubon immediately. Waiting for him to come back down the villa's long, gilded staircase, she wondered what he thought of her, an ordinary young woman in a green shirtwaist dress, who'd grinned at him but had been unable to keep the tears out of her eyes as she glanced at Kash. From the troubled, inquisitive look Audubon had given them both, she was certain he'd noticed.

She asked Kash about his father's unusual name. "No one knows his given names, not even me," Kash explained. "He'll only admit that his initials are T. S. I've always claimed that he keeps his names secret because they're silly. When I was a boy I called him Tecumseh Shirley sometimes, just to make him laugh. But he's a very private man."

"Is he the one who taught you to be cynical and aloof?"

"No, he taught me to be truthful with myself. He taught me that honor and ideals are still important. And he taught me to do my job and keep my personal problems out of it."

"But you said he's happily married."

"What does that have to do with what I said?"

"He couldn't be happily married and be as secretive as you are."

A slight smile—a sign that she'd scored a point, Rebecca thought—lightened Kash's somber expression. "He's not secretive, just private. And besides, he and I come from very different backgrounds. We have different reasons for our attitudes."

When Audubon returned, he was shaking his head in dismay, but chuckling under his breath. "Ms. Brown, come with me. Let's take a walk and discuss your situation."

Kash raised a brow but said nothing. Rebecca shot him a puzzled look and walked outside the magnificent old home with Audubon. For nearly a minute they strolled the estate's winding garden path in silence, except for his casual comments about the beauty of the oleanders and willows. Rebecca clasped her hands behind her back and waited.

Finally Audubon said, "Madame Piathip wants me to investigate you myself. She's convinced that Kash can't, or rather won't, do a proper job of it."

"Why?"

"Because she believes he's falling in love with you."

Rebecca stopped so abruptly that she slipped on the pebbled path and nearly fell down. Audubon caught her by the arm. She found her balance and stared up at him desperately. His expression was somber, but not unkind. "After listening to him rant and rave about you on the phone over the past few days—and I assure you, Rebecca, my son is *not* given to emotional outbursts—and today, seeing the way he looks at you when you're not aware of it, I think Madame Piathip may be right."

"I wish it were true."

"Do you think you could love my son?"

She searched his eyes, worried about their displeased expression. But Rebecca gave him the only answer she could. "Yes. I know that sounds outrageous, because he and I just met a few days ago, but"—she searched for words to describe the firestorm of needs and emotions Kash created in her—"but meeting him was like waking up in a world I'd never seen before, being overwhelmed and confused by it, but knowing it was where I'd always wanted to live."

"I understand." To her surprise, Audubon's expression gentled. For a moment he was distracted, as if he

were thinking of someone else. "I understand very well."
His tone was so loving that Rebecca was mesmerized.
"My wife and I had a similar circumstance. Worlds
apart, but the same."

"That's it, exactly. But Kash won't let me inside *his*
world."

Audubon's eyes became troubled again. "He's not like
any other man you'll ever meet. It will take a very special
understanding on your part to love him. Whether or not
you can break through the walls he's built will depend
on how well you understand yourself."

"How well I understand *myself*?"

He nodded. "You have to know exactly what makes a
man worth loving—the important qualities, not the
ones society taught you to appreciate. You have to be
absolutely certain."

For the first time she felt hope. "I'm certain." She said
it without hesitation, looking him straight in the eye.
He looked down at her with growing admiration, then
nodded again, appearing satisfied. He gestured toward
the path. "Then let's keep walking, and I'll try to help
you understand my son."

Kash was alarmed when Audubon came back alone.
Before he could ask why, Audubon clucked reproachfully. "I didn't put opium in her tea and leave her
sleeping in a shrub. Don't look at me that way."

"Where is she?"

"She went back to her room. She's understandably
upset. I told her Madame Piathip will never allow her to
meet Mayura, and since Mayura, being an obedient
niece, will never contradict her aunt's wishes, it's probably useless to keep trying. I also let her know that
Mayura has been in Europe all this time, waiting for the
Nalinat feud to be resolved."

Kash had a depressing vision of Rebecca packing to
go home. Audubon put a consoling hand on his arm.

"Rebecca is an innocent bystander in a muddled story we'll probably never verify. I'll do all I can to check out the details you've given me. I hope to have some information for you soon. Who knows what really happened over thirty years ago? All that matters now is that Madame Piathip is head of the Vatan family, and she says Rebecca's father was lying."

"So I should forget about Rebecca's problem and concentrate on negotiating the feud between the Vatans and Nalinats?"

"I didn't say to forget about Rebecca. Just don't expect miracles with the Vatan family. In the meantime why don't you get to know Rebecca better, and let her get to know you?"

"She'll be going back to America soon."

"So? The last time I checked a map, Iowa wasn't terribly far from Virginia. You could visit her. Or invite her to visit you. She can stay at the estate with Elena and me, if that will make you feel less threatened." Audubon smiled. "Good Lord, son, I've never thought of myself as your chaperon, but I'll certainly try."

"No. You of all people know why she and I have nothing in common. If she knew about my childhood, she'd never come near me again. She thinks it's something she could handle, but she's wrong."

Audubon took him by both shoulders. Kash and his father were nearly the same height, with Audubon only an inch taller, so they met eye-to-eye, a father and son who were only twelve years apart in age, an unlikely pair with a relationship that had often been strained, but always loving. "You left Vietnam twenty-two years ago. You were never to blame for what happened to you there. You were only a child. I thought you'd made peace with that long ago. It's been years since you and I have even discussed it."

"I've never met anyone like Rebecca before. That's why I've had to think about it again."

"People aren't shocked by these things the way they

were when you first came to America. And Rebecca certainly seems like the kind of person who'd understand."

"She'd understand," Kash agreed softly. "But deep down, it might disgust her. I couldn't stand that." He felt sick at the thought. "I won't even risk it."

"If you don't give her a chance, you'll always regret it."

"I can't make her leave, so I have no choice at the moment. But only because I'd rather she see for herself that Madame Piathip will never accept her story about being Mayura's half sister. When Rebecca admits that, she'll have to leave. And I'll let her go."

"That drawing must be incredibly difficult. I've never seen you frown so hard."

Kash's deep, teasing voice made Rebecca look up quickly from the drawing pad balanced on her knees. She was starved for the sight of him. Yesterday, after talking to Audubon, she'd needed some time alone. But now she had herself under control and could hide behind a quick smile. "Hello, Dragon."

"Hello."

He stood at the top of the path, near a small fountain that bubbled into a pool filled with gold and red fish. The breeze pushed a lock of his charcoal hair back from his high, solemn forehead, making his face look boyish in a way that tore at her heart. Though he stood with his large, capable hands shoved confidently into the pockets of tan trousers, and an open-collared tan shirt revealed the power of his dark-haired chest, he still seemed vulnerable to her.

She forgot the garden before her, the warm morning sun on her face, the trembling in her hands. The dull ache inside her chest throbbed in quiet devotion. "Flowers are harder to draw than dragons. Dragons don't have to fit anybody's imagination but my own. But flowers? Everybody knows what flowers are supposed to look like."

He walked down to the stone bench where she sat, and as he came closer, she saw the concern in his eyes. "Are you trying to be realistic these days?" he asked. "Have you given up your war on dragons?"

"No, I'm just rethinking my approach."

"Hmmm. That could mean trouble. More trouble."

"No, I'm feeling philosophical." She forced a jaunty smile and swept a hand around her at the scenery and, more important, the situation. "I'm learning to flow with the moment."

He dropped to his haunches beside the bench and looked directly into her eyes. The urge to slip her arms around his neck and kiss him very gently on the mouth was painful to resist. His troubled gaze traveled over her face. "When you stayed in your room yesterday, I didn't know what to do."

"I just needed to time to think." To her horror, tears pooled in her eyes. *I know what happened to you. But you have to tell me yourself, or it will never be all right. You have to trust me.*

Her tears heightened his distress. He reached out and stroked her shoulder soothingly. "I'm sorry my father gave you so little hope of solving this problem with the Vatan family."

He thinks I'm crying about the Vatans. She felt relieved and reassured because he didn't suspect that she and Audubon had discussed his childhood.

She cleared her throat roughly and said with grand confidence, "There's always hope. I'm betting on rainbows, not rain."

A glint of humor came into his eyes. "Every cloud has a silver lining," he intoned solemnly.

"It's always darkest before the light."

"Your glass is always half-full, not half empty."

She began to chuckle. "Be happy. Don't worry."

"Have a nice day."

They both laughed. Rebecca loved the rich, open sounds he made. She looked away, her eyes stinging again, this time with tears of poignant longing. "I guess you see that I'm not defeated yet."

"Rebecca Brown, the eternal optimist. I'm not surprised."

She swiveled toward him abruptly and blurted, "Oh, it's easy to be an optimist when nothing terrible has ever happened to you. It doesn't take such a leap of faith."

Seeing his puzzled frown, she swallowed harshly and changed the subject. "What's on the agenda for today?"

He grabbed one of her hands and stood up. Startled, she leaped up, too, and lurched against him. His swift embrace nearly undid her control, but she stepped back quickly. *Patience,* Audubon had counseled.

"I'll never win awards for grace," she admitted. "A less geeky woman might have done that on purpose. I did it because my feet are too big."

"Elephants," he said distractedly, his gaze locked on hers in a way that made her pulse race.

She blinked. "They're not *that* big."

"No, I mean that's the agenda. You need something to distract you. Something to cheer you up and make you stop thinking about your father and the Vatans. Madame Piathip has gone to her offices in the city for a few days, so you can do what you want. Would you like to take an elephant ride into the hills?"

"Sure! I'll try anything that's not embarrassing, illegal, or immoral."

"That cancels most of my plans for the day. Oh, well."

As he led her up the path at a brisk, enthusiastic pace, she stared at him in fascination. This was a side of him she'd never seen before, and she followed him more recklessly than ever.

She figured this was a small elephant, as elephants went. But from the rug-covered platform atop the animal's back, the ground seemed miles below. The owner, a young Thai man dressed in baggy cotton trousers and a brightly colored shirt, rode the elephant's neck as easily as a cowboy rides a horse. He kicked his bare heels into its shoulders occasionally, to guide it up a terraced path sheltered by magnificent rain forest.

Kash lounged with disarming ease on his side of the platform's wooden back, his long legs crossed in a lotus position, rocking comfortably with each of the animal's swaying steps. Rebecca leaned back beside him, her knees drawn up, her shoulder pressed tightly against his, her hands gripping the edges of the seat.

"Where did you learn to ride elephants?" she asked wryly. "Are there classes for this in Asia? Like driver's ed?"

"You have to believe that you won't fall off. Then you can relax. Confidence is simply a matter of trusting your elephant."

"There's a moral in that, somewhere."

"Relax, Becca. Enjoy the scenery."

Becca. He'd remembered the nickname he'd given her in bed the other night. Surprise and delight warmed her. Rebecca realized abruptly that she was grinning and he was watching her. "I'm glad I could cheer you up," he said, but sounded puzzled.

"I trust my elephant," she said, deadpan.

The land rose in a beautiful panorama of wide terraces dotted with rice paddies. The shimmering emerald ponds stair-stepped down the hillsides, while above them the shadowy forest beckoned with the crooked limbs of enormous, gnarled trees. The elephant nimbly followed an invisible path into the woodland, and eventually arrived at a glen overlooking the terraces.

At its trainer's instructions the elephant knelt. Kash jumped off and held up his arms to Rebecca. She decided she could learn to love riding elephants, considering the fringe benefits. She put her hands on

Kash's broad shoulders and inhaled softly as his hands settled on her waist.

The intensity in his eyes hypnotized her as he lifted her down. For one wonderful second she was against his torso as he set her on the ground, with her head tilted back and her gaze locked on his. Nothing else existed except him.

"I will set up lunch," the owner said cheerfully, untying a bamboo hamper behind the platform's seat.

Kash let her go, and she busied herself smoothing her lose green shorts and top. When the driver had placed a colorful blanket and the hamper's contents on the soft forest floor, he made a *wai* and went to eat lunch with his elephant, tethered a dozen yards away.

She sat down beside Kash and looked hungrily at rice delicacies wrapped in banana leaves, bamboo tubes stuffed with baked seafood and vegetables, and cups of sliced fruit with coconut cream. "This is the most fantastic meal I've ever seen."

He popped a piece of fresh pineapple into her mouth. His fingertips brushed her lips. She forgot about the pineapple dripping sweetly on her tongue and drew her lips together. Without planning it, she sucked his fingers lightly as he pulled them away.

His hand stopped in midair. He looked startled and hypnotized at the same time. Rebecca was captured by the spell between him and her. She stared back at him in wonder, while inside she dissolved into helpless desire.

Kash took a deep breath, then abruptly distracted himself by arranging food on thick linen napkins. "Did Leon ever tell you that you could set his plaid sports coat on fire with a technique like that one?"

She laughed shakily. "No, but one time he said I was a good, clean date with no bad habits."

"That was the most romantic compliment he could think of?"

"Yes. It pretty much summed up our relationship."

"You've developed some wonderful bad habits since you ditched Leon."

"I had a great teacher, Mr. Santelli."

"Me? I said I'd civilize you, not teach you to make naughty with my fingers."

"And I said I'd turn you into a wholesome dragon. We've both failed so far. But there's plenty of time. Lunch is just getting started."

"I think I'll move to the far side of the blanket."

"Coward. I won't bite."

"Your lips are dangerous enough. Don't bring your teeth into this argument too."

She leaned toward him. "A brave man loves a challenge."

He picked up another piece of pineapple and eyed her thoughtfully. The arousal darkening his eyes made her ache to touch him. Rebecca gave him a small, saucy wink. "You asked for trouble. Now what are you going to do about it?"

He exhaled slowly. A dam of restraint seemed about to break inside him. "Feed it some pineapple, and see what happens next."

He lifted his hand to her mouth.

Trembling, she parted her lips.

And suddenly the day exploded with gunshots.

Rebecca screamed. Bullets zipped overhead, snapping leaves off the trees, tearing bark from the tree trunks. The elephant bolted back in the direction of home, with his lithe owner clambering aboard his neck and clinging desperately.

"Get down!" Kash shoved Rebecca to the blanket and flattened himself on top of her. They lay there, breathing heavily, and listening to the forest. There were no more shots, but birds screeched in alarm. Their transportation had disappeared. Kash cursed softly under his breath, feathering her ear with terse, raw words. "I should have brought a gun. Dammit, I was careless."

"Shh. This is nuts. Who'd have thought anyone would bother us?"

"I'm supposed to be protecting you. *Dammit.*" She'd never heard such fury and tension in his voice before. She thought she felt his heart beating powerfully against her back. Her own heart pounded a furious rhythm. "You *are* protecting me," she joked weakly. "If the elephant comes back, he'll step on you first."

"We can't stay here. We've got to find some cover. Follow me."

He pulled her to her feet. Crouching, they ran down the hillside and leaped onto a terrace. She ran behind him along a narrow strip of land between two small rice paddies. They zigzagged down the hill, splashing through ponds, slipping on the soft, wet earth. Another shot zipped over their heads as they dived into the foliage at the base of the hill.

She fell into mud and slick, clinging plants. Kash immediately dropped beside her and slid an arm around her waist. "You okay, Corn Blossom?"

Rebecca wiped mud from her lips. "Never happier, Dragon."

"Good. Let's keep moving. We'll take the long way back, and confuse them.

"Look out!"

She shot a hand forward and snatched an orange snake that was coiling near his free arm. Clutching it behind the head, she flung it in a long arch. It landed nearly a dozen feet away.

Kash exploded with anger. "Dammit, don't grab everthing that moves around here! That snake might have been poisonous." Then he cupped her head toward him and kissed her grimy mouth.

She gave him a shaky smile. "Grabbing snakes got me a kiss. Sucking your fingers didn't. You're a strange man."

"A crazy man. And it's your fault. Come on."

On hands and knees they crawled deeper into the

forest, then got up and sprinted through the trees. He stopped her before her breath gave out completely, and pulled her to him. Rebecca leaned against him gratefully. Her face rested against the center of his heaving chest, where his shirt was open enough to allow his sweat and matted chest hair to tickle her cheek. She found the feel and scent of him comforting, and from the way he held her, she suspected he liked the reassurance too.

"Rest. We have a long way to go," he said softly. "No more running."

"No more running," she agreed, tilting her head back and looking at him calmly.

"You aren't afraid?"

"No. I trust my elephant."

He began to laugh.

Eight

They arrived at the Vatan estate long after midnight. Bewildered servants stared at them as they trudged through the foyer, exhausted and dirty. Kash told someone to bring food to his suite. To Rebecca, he said, "Why don't you take a bath, then come to my room? I'm going to make some phone calls."

She nodded, too tired to speak.

In her room she dropped her damp, muddy clothes and ruined tennis shoes on the floor, then climbed into a hot bath filled with cinnamon crystals and thick white suds. After halfheartedly scrubbing herself, she put her head back on the tub's wide marble rim and fell asleep.

She awoke quickly when a hand touched her head. Kash was sitting on the floor beside the tub. She could see a black silk robe over his bare chest. His black hair, still a little damp from his bath, glistened in the soft overhead lamps. A thin red scratch ran across the bridge of his nose, giving it a more brutal appeal. In contrast, his fingers were very gentle as he stroked a strand of her wet hair away from her forehead and studied her with concern. "When you didn't come to my suite, I was worried."

She glanced down at the suds that covered her like a

fluffy white blanket. They lapped at her breasts just above the nipples, a fact she was vividly aware of. "How are you?" she asked huskily. "You must be sleepy too."

He nodded. "But I have too many questions to ask. I've already made some calls to my people. They'll see what they can learn about what happened today."

"Do you think the Nalinats are responsible?"

"Probably. They like scare tactics. They're harmless, but effective."

"Man, are they."

"Ready to give up?"

"Nope. I'm scared, not chicken."

He smiled. "The unsinkable Rebecca Brown."

"I'm mad too. I want to meet these Nalinat creeps and ask some point-blank questions."

He shook his head. "They'd only be insulted. We'll have to make some decisions later. It may take time. Nothing happens fast in this part of the world. Try to relax."

"I might as well. I'm so tired, I can barely think."

"Me too. That's dangerous."

"Or tempting."

"Both."

In the silence that followed, she felt as if the water were growing hotter with each second. There was so much she wanted to say to him. Tenderness and gratitude mingled with desire. Her throat was too tight for speech. He remained kneeling beside the tub, his fingers caressing the side of her face. Restraint and bittersweet dilemma radiated from his troubled expression.

"We did well together," he said in a voice so low she had to read his lips to understand the words. Her hearing aid lay somewhere in the forest near the rice paddies. "You made it feel natural to be a team."

"Good for me," she whispered. The breath had stalled in her chest. Every fiber in her body cried out for him.

His lips barely moved. "I should go."

A broken sound burst from her throat. "*Don't*. Please, don't."

"If I stay, I'll—"

"You'll make me happy. And I'll try to make you happy." She laid a hand along the side of his face. Emotion glistened in his eyes. "Give me a chance. Give yourself a chance."

They moved together, she reaching up, he reaching down. She rose out of the water to put her arms around him as he lifted her over the tub's pale gold rim. Suds slid down her naked body and were absorbed by his black robe. He was already kissing her by the time he laid down beside her on the richly carpeted floor. She opened his robe, then pressed herself to his bare chest.

His fingers drifted up and down her side, stroking her from shoulder to thigh, then flattening around the indention of her waist to pull her closer. She mewled into his hot, searching mouth, as sensations gathered inside her like a star about to burst. Exploring his chest with trembling hands, she stroked the hard points of his nipples, traced the corded muscles along his rib cage, then drew her hands upward and clasped them behind his neck.

His chest hair was as soft as lamb's wool against her tender breasts, and his thighs, covered in the robe's silk magic, tantalized hers with each small flexing of his body. When he smoothed his hand over her water-slick hips, she quivered wildly. He drew back and looked deeply into her eyes as his hand caressed her, moving under her, cupping her, touching her intimately with such perfect skill that each stroke of his fingers made sensations shoot through her womb.

"Becca," he murmured roughly, his voice a compelling invitation. His face was flushed and savage with restraint, but his eyes glowed with infinite patience.

Her feminine instincts welcomed him, her sighs, her body's smooth, sleek yearning under his hand, the frantic kisses she placed on his chest and neck. They settled on their sides, facing each other. Untying his robe, she watched one side slip down. The other she pushed with tantalizing slowness up to his lean, angular hip. Then she smoothed her hand on the taut skin and let the silky material cascade down behind him.

Her first sight of his uncovered body brought a sense of wonder. His golden, masculine beauty combined with the primal thrust of his arousal to make her reach for him in awe, her hands feathering over his stomach and down his abdomen, while the rough cadence of his breath told her he was on fire.

She cuddled his hot satin hardness in her palm, marveling at the contrasts. Touching him made her light-headed with anticipation. He tilted her head back, then kissed her with erotic abandon, as if he wanted to taste all of her through her mouth. She cried out with delight.

Need and affection pulsed together in a slow, breathtaking rhythm between them. He got to his knees and bent over her, pulling her into an arch, with his hands under her back. His mouth descended on the taut skin of her stomach. She writhed happily and helplessly under the sweet sucking motion of his lips.

Rebecca thought she'd die with pleasure as he covered her body with those same sensual kisses, lavishing them on her breasts, tickling them across her thighs, then, finally, when she was already losing control in a storm of desire, parting her thighs and delving between them.

She cried out in astonishment at the most searing pleasure in the world, more exquisite than anything she'd ever imagined. It stole her thoughts and consumed her with waves of primitive hunger, and at the same moment, blinding joy. She whispered Kash's name over and over. He swept her into his arms while she was still calling him, then lifted her and stood.

He strode into the other room, darkened except for faint starlight gleaming in the window. "Becca, hold me," he urged hoarsely, as he placed her on the bed. "I'm so broken up inside that I don't know what I'm doing. Nothing's ever been so perfect in my life before."

"You're doing just fine," she answered in a voice that vibrated with love. "And I'll hold you so tight, I'll keep you together."

He stripped his robe off and lowered himself into her outstretched arms. Slowly easing his body between her thighs, he brushed kisses over her mouth and made promises with careful caresses. His larger, more muscular body hinted at the power to hurt, to take selfishly, to control. But she wasn't surprised by his gentleness, by the way he reassured her with his gracefulness while exciting her with his size and strength.

Trembling again, she stroked his hair and looked up into his face as he cupped her hips to him and posed on the threshold of joining.

"I never thought I could make *love* to anyone," he murmured. "But now I know I can." A single tear slid down his cheek. She moaned softly and arched her head up to kiss it. "Don't stop," she ordered gently. "You're a natural."

She slid her hands down his back. He listened ecstatically as she told him with eager caresses and soft, half-spoken words that there was nothing but pleasure in his slow, careful merger with her body.

Rebecca was lost in the beauty of that fulfillment. She held him as tightly as she had promised. She kept him together body and soul. In the enchanted moments that followed, he showed her how a man could be more than he'd been born to be, and all that a woman could want.

The morning air was kissing him. Warm and smelling of cinnamon, it moved across his dreamscape, feathering his lips, making him smile. Luscious memories crept back. Glimmers of a long, emotion-filled night of passion. He remembered intervals of blissful half-sleep mingled with torrid awakenings, caressing hands learning to please him more each time, sweetness surrounding him, pulsing with his own life force, soft cries of feminine delight echoing his own masculine ones.

He also remembered the relaxed conversations, whispered in the darkness. He had given away pieces of himself that he'd been unwilling to share with anyone before. They were so simple and yet so fragile. Daydreams. Hobbies. Small human likes and dislikes. All night the dreamer beside him had listened, then trusted him with her own delicate whimsies. Now she was telling him it hadn't been a dream after all.

Rebecca. *Becca*. He loved her. The words for it were encased in a cold shell inside him, and he didn't know if he could ever tell her. He doubted he could ever tell her why it was impossible. If he told her, the innocent bond between them would never be the same.

But for now, as the morning kissed him with such easy devotion, hope was too tempting to resist. He pushed aside the darkness and opened his eyes.

"Good morning," she whispered, gazing down at him from under sexily tousled brunette hair. Her blue eyes were sleepy and sultry, filled with the night's memories and the day's anticipation. Desire rocketed through him.

"*Great* morning," he corrected. "The best."

Her pleased smile made happiness rise in his chest and took the raw edge off his surge of arousal. There would be no turbulent rush to join together this time, though it had been like that once or twice during the night, when the mood was wild. This time would be infinitely slow and spiritual, a long sigh of harmony instead of a shout.

"Be still," she ordered mildly. Resting one hand against his cheek, she lightly brushed her fingertip over his lashes. He watched her study them with fascination, then grin. "I couldn't do this in the dark. I've been wanting to touch them for days."

"Why?"

"Because I love the way the tips curl. Like a little boy's." She scrutinized them solemnly.

Kash wasn't the kind of man who wanted to hear that his eyelashes were boyish. If anyone else had said so, he'd have scowled in secret embarrassment. "And all this time I thought it was my incredible body you wanted." But he couldn't keep from chuckling.

"Well, they're attached to your body. I want everything."

Kash felt the darkness again. *That's what I'm afraid of.* But he ignored it by taking her in his arms and abruptly rolling her over. He lost himself in the love glowing in her eyes. "Now, let me take a good, long look at *your* eyelashes. Then I'll work my way down."

"Hmmm, I like that plan."

He began kissing her, brushing his lips over her eyes, causing her to make a noise halfway between a chuckle and a sexy purr. "How are you this morning?" he asked. Carefully he slid his hand down her belly, cherishing her small quiver and the way she arched to encourage his caress.

"Wonderful," she whispered.

"But maybe a little tender?"

"Filled with the most incredible tenderness," she answered huskily.

He nuzzled her neck but gave her a rebuking look. "I meant the other kind. Be honest. I tried very hard to remember that you'd never been with a man before, but I'm afraid I was, hmmm, *overwhelmed* by your enthusiasm."

Though she grinned at him, he felt her move gingerly when he stroked his hand over the soft mound at the top of her legs. "Okay, pardner, you caught me," she intoned in a comical cowboy drawl. "I confess." But her blue eyes didn't have any humor in them. They watched him worriedly, "Don't run scared, pardner. I may be a little saddle sore, but I'm still the best bronco buster this side of Bangkok. *Bangkok.* If'n I was a tenderfoot, I'd make a joke about that there name. But hey, I ain't a tenderfoot. What's tender is about a leg-length higher up."

He bent his head over her and laughed until his sides ached. She put her arms around him tightly. "There are so many ways to make love. I'd really like to touch you and talk to you. Would you mind if that's all we do this morning?"

Kash drew his head up quickly and looked at her. "Of course not. Do you seriously think I'm upset? I'm having the time of my life."

"I don't know what to think, right now. I'm hopeful, but worried. I don't want to push you too hard or say the wrong thing. I guess I'm afraid you'll tell me that what happened last night was wrong, and you don't want to be this involved with me."

"No. I can't predict that will happen to you and me after this situation with the Vatan family is resolved, but I'll tell you this. You'll leave me. I won't leave you."

"Kash!" Obviously bewildered and upset, she took his face between her hands and studied him as if she could draw his secrets out with her willpower.

"Don't," he ordered softly, shaking his head.

"Your lack of faith is the only thing that would ever drive me away," she told him in a low, anguished voice. "Until you can tell me *why* you and I could never have a life together, I won't feel that you trust me."

"Becca, I trust you in a way I've never trusted anyone else. Believe me."

"We're having a little of a communication problem," she told him, frowning gently. "Everything's changed between us since yesterday." She added in a pensive tone, "I suspect you regret that a little."

Kash felt a flood of sadness and doubt, not about his feelings for her, but about the future. He was a loner even where religion was concerned, but now he thought gratefully about the Buddhist belief in living life one moment at a time. They sought their paradise, their nirvana, by blocking out the past and future. He pulled Rebecca closer to him and said as lightly as he could, "I regret only one thing."

"What?"

"That you can't hear well out of this ear." He put his head beside hers and whispered, *I love you, I love you forever.*

"Stop. Use the other side, I want to hear," she demanded, sinking her hands into his hair. She lifted his head and scowled at him mildly. "What did you say?"

"Something shocking. I could hardly put it into words."

"Then show me."

Kash took her deeper into his arms. "That should be easy."

Madame Piathip stayed in the city for several days, and without her suspicious scrutiny, Rebecca could forget about the Vatan family and enjoy being with Kash. Making love with him opened up a universe of sensations and emotions she'd never felt before, and every day was full of new adventures, new intimacies.

But one dawn she woke up alone in his stately bedroom. Her mind still hummed with delicious memories of the night before. He'd carried her to bed after a flirtatious game of chess. She'd never known that the game could be so sexy.

Looking around curiously, Rebecca climbed out of his bed, peered into the bath, called his name plaintively, then noticed a note on a small table by the door.

If you wake up before I return, I'm at the small shrine near the pond. Please come. Kash.

She dressed in a brightly embroidered green tunic and flowing white silk pants, pulled her hair back with a black ribbon, put sturdy black slippers on her feet, and hurried outside. The light was rosy and golden.

Dew hung on the thick forest beyond the estate's stone walls and stained the walls with dark patterns. The air smelled of flowers and damp grass. Inhaling deeply, she went down the path to the pond at a quick, swinging walk.

He was seated on the far side of the garden's pond, in front of a serene female statue made of white stone. The goddess held both a lotus blossom and a jar. The jar was turned downward, as if pouring. Rebecca came to a stop several yards behind Kash, catching her breath at the handsome and tranquil sight he made, his perfect stillness. His arms rested lightly on his knees, and his head was bowed.

His torso was covered in a simple white shirt of cotton that clung to the sculpted contours of his broad shoulders and strong back. Loose black trousers emphasized his long, lean legs. He was barefoot. A wisp of morning breeze lifted strands of his black hair. At the base of the shrine was a stone cup, and in it he'd placed several sticks of incense. The breeze wafted their faint gray smoke upward.

Poignant understanding swelled in her chest. He was a complex combination of cultures and attitudes. Physically large and powerful—very Western in that way—but filled with a vulnerable grace that struck her as humble, reverent, and very Eastern.

Not wanting to break the spell, she kept quiet and started to sit down, but her foot snapped a twig on the grass. Kash raised his head and turned to look at her. His expression was so troubled that she bit back a sound of distress. His serenity had been a facade. As she went to him, he made a painful-looking effort to appear casual. "Good morning," he said, reaching up a hand.

"Good morning," she answered in awkward Vietnamese.

"You remembered our little vocabulary lesson last night."

"You've taught me a lot over the past few days." She took his hand and sat down beside him. "You're a good teacher."

"You're an inspiring student."

"For a barbarian, as Madame Piathip might say." He put his arm around her, but there was something distant and stiff about his posture. Rebecca stroked a fingertip along the shadow under one of his eyes. "You didn't sleep very well."

He smiled. "Only because I kept waking up to nuzzle the naked barbarian woman who kept pressing herself against me. But why should last night be any different from the others?"

"Because you usually sleep soundly in between nuzzlings. I know, because sometimes I watch you."

"Oh? Is that your hobby?"

"Yep. I whisper commands into your ears. You know, like subliminal messages."

"What commands?"

"It's a secret. But you're responding nicely, so it must work. Except I'll have to fix this little problem of yours. No more slipping out of bed without waking me up."

"I had a promise to keep." He nodded toward the incense and the Buddhist statue. "In Vietnam they call her Quan-Am. She represents compassion. Her jar pours the water of compassion on believers. She helps a person find the compassion inside himself. I'm not a Buddhist, but I appreciate the idea."

Rebecca nodded, watching him closely. He tried to hide his mysterious grief, but she felt it. "Did you come here to find compassion for yourself, or for someone else?"

"Someone else. Someone who died twenty-six years ago today."

"Please tell me. At least tell me as much as you're comfortable sharing."

He searched her eyes with a long, intense gaze. She

could see the conflict inside him, and it tore at her. "Are you talking about your mother?" she asked softly.

He shut his eyes for a moment, and she thought he wasn't going to answer. But when he opened them, they were calm. "Yes."

"Please. Tell me anything you can about her. If there are ugly memories you don't want to talk about, that's fine. Just tell me the good things."

He exhaled wearily. "She did her best with what she was given. Her father was an Egyptian diplomat who had business ties in Vietnam back when the French controlled the country. Her mother was a mandarin's daughter. Because she was mixed-blood and illegitimate, she had very little chance of marrying well or finding a good job."

"You mean she was a social outcast, like the Amerasian children our soldiers left behind?"

"Yes. Her mother's family took care of her, but they were killed during the war with the French, back in the fifties. She was just a girl when she was orphaned. After that, she did the best she could."

Rebecca reached across his lap and took his clenched hand. She wound her fingers through his. "How did she manage?"

Kash's hard black gaze bored into her. "I remember her singing to me, and teaching me to play games, and protecting me, because I was even more of an outcast than she was."

Rebecca looked up at him steadily. He was evading the question. In a matter-of-fact tone she said, "Because your father was American?"

"Yes. He was an army intelligence officer. Hell, for all I know, he might have worked for the CIA. He was one of the advisers who came to Vietnam about 1960. He was killed a few years later. That's all I learned about him."

"Tell me about your childhood. You said to me once that you spent it fighting and stealing, to survive."

"That's right. My mother died when I was about five.

Audubon discovered me a few years later. He was a soldier, one of those idealistic college boys who'd come to Vietnam to save the world. He couldn't save the world, but he saved me."

Abruptly Kash dropped his arm from around her, brought her hand to his mouth for a hard kiss, then announced, "End of story. I came to the shrine today to burn incense on the anniversary of my mother's death. The Vietnamese place a lot of importance on honoring ancestors. I perform this ceremony every year to remember the small part of me that's Vietnamese. And for my mother."

Tell me the rest. You have to tell me, she implored silently. He looked down at her as if reading her mind. "That's all, Becca."

"Please talk to me."

"I've told you all that's important about that part of my life."

"Except what makes you so different from every other man I've known. Except what makes it impossible for you to believe I love you."

He inhaled sharply and raised a hand. "Don't ever say that to me again. I certainly won't say it to you."

"I thought we'd gotten beyond that barrier in the past few days."

"No, we've danced close to it, that's all."

"You said I'd leave you. You didn't mention that I'd leave you only because you'd *force* me to."

"Listen to me." He swiveled to face her and took her by both shoulders in a rough grip. "My work keeps me on the move most of the time. This month I'm in Thailand. Next month I may be in Europe. The month after that I could be in South America. I have a home near my father's in Virginia, but I'm hardly ever there. What are you going to do—sit in Iowa and wait for me to breeze by for an occasional visit?"

"You're putting up smoke screens."

"I'm never going to come home from work each day

and sit in a lounge chair watching my wife make needlepoint finger towels for the church bazaar while the kids do their homework and the dog snores. I wouldn't know how to fit in."

"I wouldn't either, since I don't do needlepoint, have no kids and no dog, snoring or otherwise. I thought the whole point of making a life with someone was to start from the ground up, then work out something special and unique. If you were a cartoonist, I'd tell you that your characters are stick people, and you've got no imagination. You're trying to draw the punch line before you've sketched the first panel."

"I'm painting the picture the only way I can see it."

"Did I ask you to marry me?" she asked angrily, getting to her knees. "Did I ask you to trade in any part of your life for part of mine? *No.* So why are you forcing this discussion? I'm not going to beat my chest and tear out my hair when you leave me. Oh, yes, you'll leave *me,* because you'll never admit that you hate being alone."

She grabbed a fresh stick of incense, held it against the burning ones, and when it began to smoke, laid it at the shrine's base. Looking up into Quan-Am's smiling face, Rebecca held out her hands in supplication. "Please, give Kash some compassion for himself."

"Stop it," Kash ordered.

"And please let him understand that I didn't fall in love with him to change what he is, or what he comes from."

"I said stop," he repeated, getting up and pulling her with him. Half crying now, she twisted in his harsh embrace and looked up at him bitterly. "What happened to you when you were a child? You have to trust me enough to tell me. Please, Kash. Please."

"Mr. Kash, Mr. Kash," a nervous male voice called from the direction of the house. The person was hidden by trees and shrubs along the winding path. "Where are you? Come quick!"

He stepped back and released her. "I have to go."

"You have to hide."

"Call it hiding, if you want to."

"I'll be in my room," she told him wearily. "I shouldn't have come here this morning. Your ceremony shouldn't have been ruined with a pointless argument."

"The ceremony's over. It's time to get back to real life. You're my only concern. I've got to get this Vatan mess settled and get you out of here."

And out of your life, she thought. His words stung so much that she didn't ask him to elaborate. Again the servant's voice cut through the morning. "Please, Mr. Kash, come quick! And bring Miss Brown with you! It's an emergency!"

Frowning, Kash took her hand. They ran back to the house. A manservant was waiting at the top of the path, wringing his hands. He made a jerky *wai* in greeting. "The police are here, sir!"

"They want to see me?"

"They want to see Miss Brown! They say Madame Piathip sent them!"

Rebecca felt Kash's hand tighten possessively on her own. He frowned in bewilderment. "Did Madame return from Bangkok last night?"

"No, she's still at her house in the city."

Kash turned toward Rebecca. She looked up at him with strangled anxiety. "What does she intend to do— have me deported?"

"Whatever it is, don't worry. The problem can be fixed with talk or money."

But the stern police captain who waited for them with several of his officers in the house's front hall didn't look interested in negotiating. "Miss Brown, you're accused of stealing jewelry," he said in crisp, formal English. "You'll have to come with us."

Rebecca shook her head numbly. "Jewelry? What jewelry?" Kash stepped between her and the police officer, his face fierce with restraint, his body as taut as a shield. "Madame has made a mistake. Please, let's discuss this privately. You and I can determine where the mistake was made, I'm sure."

"No discussion," the captain retorted. "Madame Vatan accuses this woman of stealing a jade earring inscribed to her dead sister." To Rebecca he said, "You will give me this earring, please."

Rebecca slipped past Kash and faced the man firmly. "I sent that earring to Madame Vatan to prove my relationship to her family. She returned the earring to me when I came here as her guest."

"I was in charge of the arrangement," Kash added. "There was no theft."

The captain only scowled. "Madam Vatan says the earring was stolen from her many years ago. She's taken the past few days to decide whether to press charges. Now she has."

Rebecca trembled with anger. "But that's not true! The earring belonged to my father! It was a keepsake! I inherited it."

Kash angled in front of her again. "Miss Brown had nothing to do with any theft."

The captain unyielding stance became stiffer. "That will be determined later. She must come with us. She'll be held in jail until this is resolved."

Rebecca's imagination went into overdrive. She pictured a dungeon with large roaches and sadistic lady wardens, like a bad drive-in movie she'd once seen, only with Thai actors instead of Americans. Her knees turned weak, and she leaned suddenly against Kash, gasping for breath. He caught her around the shoulders as she righted herself. His chest moved roughly under the hand she wound into his shirtfront. "I'll go with her," he said. "There's no point in putting her in jail. I'll vouch for her."

"Who are you? Just an American who thinks he's one of us because he's mixed-blood. Just a mongrel. You have no authority here."

"You're not taking her to jail," Kash said evenly.

Rebecca realized that he was on the verge of violence, and she sensed that the situation was only going to get worse unless she changed it. She forced herself to smile and patted Kash's chest. "Hey, cool it." He looked down at her with grim surprise. She smiled wider, though her stomach was jumping with nervousness. "I came here for adventure, you know? To boldly go where no cartoonist has gone before. I've already been kidnapped and shot at. Going to jail is the logical next step."

As he searched her eyes, she made herself nod reassuringly. "It'll be interesting. Really. We're not getting anything accomplished this way, so let's stop arguing and head for the pokey. The slammer. The old hoosegow. I'll visit with the other inmates while you work on getting me out."

Kash didn't look convinced. The captain interjected, "If you don't cooperate, I'll arrest you, too, and then you won't be much help to Miss Brown."

Kash looked at if he wanted to tear someone apart. Rebecca's thoughts churned with fear, confusion, and devotion. He was the ultimate protector, and she loved him more wildly than ever. But in a small, desolate part of her mind was the knowledge that none of this meant anything, that the words he'd spoken at the shrine only minutes earlier had been serious. He might protect and save her a thousand times, but in the end he would push her away.

"Let me go," she said in a soft, broken voice. "I'll be fine."

He released her by inches, his jaw clenched and eyes black with fury as he gazed past her at the captain. "I'll follow in a separate car."

"Do whatever you wish," the captain answered, and shrugged. He took Rebecca's arm. "You're officially under arrest, Miss Brown."

Nine

Madame Piathip sat in her modern offices high above Bangkok, looking masterful in a blue business suit, a silver-haired tyrant with her own sincere but frustrating reasons for what she'd done. "How else could I show her that my family will never believe her father's story?" Madame asked plaintively. "Her father must have stolen the earring when he lived here. I've been thinking about her story for days. I'm convinced that explains how he acquired the earring."

Kash paced the floor, too furious to sit down as he should have, too worried about Rebecca to care about politeness. "But you know that Rebecca didn't steal it."

"But she did! She inherited it! It's the same thing!"

Kash halted and faced her formally. "You've made your point. Now please use your connections to have her released."

"No. Let a judge hear her case. Let her stay in an unpleasant jail cell until then, and meditate about her mistakes."

"There's no evidence against her."

Madame shrugged. "I know, but maybe she'll be so tired of bothering us that she'll go home as soon as she's released."

"It could be weeks or even months before her case is heard."

Madame smiled impishly. "She'll learn patience, then."

Kash boiled with anger. Through gritted teeth he said as calmly as he could, "If you'll have her released, I'll guarantee that she won't pursue her story about being Mayura's half sister."

"Oh? How will you do that?"

He bowed ironically. "I have a certain amount of control over her."

"Hmmph. I don't trust you anymore. You've fallen in love with her!"

"No."

"Yes! It shows in everything you say and do concerning her!" Madame Piathip leaned forward, her eyes narrowing. "I will not drop my charge against her. She stays in jail."

"Then consider this the end of my work for you. I'll call my people in Switzerland immediately. I suggest you find someone else to take care of Mayura there and to negotiate with the Nalinats here."

"You can't do this! My old friend Audubon won't desert me! He'll insist that you stay!"

"My father was your husband's friend, not yours. Don't expect him to approve of your revenge against an innocent person."

"You'd leave my niece unprotected in a foreign country just to impress that clumsy, boring American woman? Where is your honor?"

"Rebecca has been thrown into a Bangkok jail. She's the one who needs protection at the moment. Don't ever forget, Madame, that I can be ruthless when it's needed. That's one reason you hired me."

"The truth is, you can be ruthless because you've betrayed our contract! I didn't hire you to fall in love with that woman!"

"That has nothing to do with this argument. I'll never stand by and let an innocent person be abused."

"You love her, admit it! What a fool you are! Do you think a respectable woman could ever love *you*?"

"I didn't ask her to love me. Her problem isn't personal to me. I wouldn't sanction your tactics or your lack of decency against any innocent person, not just Rebecca. I don't understand your motives, and I've begun to suspect them. I have doubts about everything you've told me. I'm going to get some truthful answers."

"There are no hidden motives here except your own! Your own blind belief that you can impress that woman so much that she won't care what you are!" Madame Piathip lowered her voice and hissed, "I *know* what you are! The son of a whore, and yourself a—"

"Good afternoon." He bowed and made a respectful *wai* to her. Inside he was deadly calm. His ability to shut off his emotions had come into play for self-preservation. Now he could proceed with his plans to help Rebecca. "Whatever else I am, I'm now the man you should fear most."

Her stunned silence followed him as he left the office.

Shoo, Rebecca ordered silently, then clutched the edge of the bamboo mat on which she lay and watched a rat scurry through the bars of the cell. Dim light filtered in from a ceiling fixture out in the hall, making the rat look shadowy and sinister. This wasn't a fat small-town rat, minding its own business, this was a hungry urban rat. She pictured a cartoon rodent with tattoos and tiny little brass knuckles and a bad attitude. At that moment her real live rat headed toward the other five women in the small cell, sniffing at their bare feet. Rebecca lurched upright. "Shoo! Scat!"

It halted, raised up on its hind legs, and bared its teeth at her. The other women stirred quickly, looked around, and kicked at the rat, which leisurely crawled out of the cell. "You worry too much," one of them said to her, not unkindly. The young woman wore a tight, short dress, now stained with dirt and sweat. Her long black hair was tangled, and her face was dirty. But it was a delicate, intelligent face with beautiful eyes. She was the only Thai cellmate who spoke English. In the two days since Rebecca's arrival, the girl had watched her warily but said very little.

"The rat is gone," the girl said patiently. "Stop shivering. He's only trying to make a living." She hesitated. "What is *shoo*? What is *scat*?"

"Magic Iowa words."

Slowly Rebecca's muscles relaxed to their constant level of tension. Shoo? she thought giddily. Scat? She laughed to cover the desperation clawing at her throat, then leaned against the cool stone wall, hugging her knees to her chest. The girl sat up and leaned beside her. They were about the same age, Rebecca guessed. Both barefoot, both dirty. Rebecca tucked the tail of her tunic around her hips and remembered how pretty it had been two days ago. Where was Kash? She'd gone through a thousand different horrors in the past two days, wondering where he was. Couldn't he have found a way to see her or at least send a message?

She thought back to his harsh words. He'd made it clear that there was nothing permanent about their relationship. But he'd also said that when they parted, it would be her choice, not his.

"What law did you break?" her companion asked.

"The law that says mild-mannered cartoonists should be satisfied with dull lives." Rebecca smiled pensively at her. Looking bewildered, she smiled back. "I'm accused of stealing a piece of jewelry. I didn't do it."

"Isn't anyone coming to get you out? You're an American, after all."

Rebecca swallowed hard. "Someone's supposed to be working on my case. I hope he hasn't forgotten me. What about you? What did you do?"

"Made an important man angry. So this is my punishment. I'll get out in a few weeks, maybe. He told them I stole from him. I didn't. I just kept money that ought to be mine. I earned it."

"What kind of work do you do?"

"I work at a bar." The girl's black lashes fluttered with awkwardness. She looked away and added coolly, "You wouldn't understand."

"I'll try. Tell me about it. How long have you worked there?"

"Many years. I was sold to the owner by my family."

"Why?"

"My parents needed money. They had too many daughters."

"Can't you leave?"

"Not unless I pay back my price. That's hard to do. I have two children to raise."

"Who's taking care of your children now?"

The girl's lip trembled. "One of the others who works there.

Rebecca hesitated, wondering how the girl would react, then took her hand. The girl flinched and looked at her askance. "What do you want?"

"Nothing. Just somebody to talk to. My name is Rebecca."

Wide-eyed, the girl said slowly, "I'm Rungsima."

"Tell me about your work."

"It would only shock you."

"No, it would only make me understand. I want to understand."

"You're different. Not afraid of anything." She smiled. "Except rats."

Rebecca shook her head. "I'm afraid of everything right now. I'm so scared, I can hardly stand it. I'm discouraged, and depressed, and nothing makes any sense."

"Then you're not so different from me." They huddled closer together. Rebecca refused to cry, but her chest filled with aching despair. She'd never been trapped before, never felt like a piece of property, and never been so helpless. It hurt worse because she thought of Kash and for the first time understood the forces that had turned him into a man who couldn't let anyone own him, even with love.

"I'm bribing people right and left," Kash told Audubon over the phone. "If I don't get to see her soon, I'm going to have myself arrested just to be near her."

"Dammit, son, you've pushed me too far. I'll send Traynor to stop you. If he has to use force, he will. I've never heard you talk this way before. Don't let emotion ruin what you're trying to do. This is the first time I've had to worry about your judgment."

Kash paced his apartment, feeling frantic. "How would you feel if you hadn't been able to save Elena? If she'd been taken back to Russia? Or if she were in jail?"

"I'd be crazy with worry, but I'd make myself think calmly. One wrong step and the police could keep her, and you, locked up for a long time."

"I won't make a wrong step."

"Don't do anything reckless. There's a lot more at stake here than you realize. If you'll give me a chance, I'll tell you what we just found out."

"The only thing at stake here is getting my personal Mary Poppins out of hell."

"*Listen to me.* Madame Piathip, damn her coy little heart, may have been lying to you about everything. Rebecca probably is Mayura's half sister. I suspect that Mayura doesn't even know it. If I'm right, it's been a family secret for almost thirty years."

"What's been a secret?"

"I had Traynor investigate your art smuggler, the one who claimed that Reverend Brown was involved in something illegal, and that he never married a Thai woman or had a child by one. Madame Piathip threatened the man. He's elderly; he lied to you to protect his past history from investigation. She set you up."

Kash cursed darkly. "Did the man know Reverend Brown at all?"

"Yes, but only because Rebecca's father started an orphanage for Thai children, and the art smuggler wanted to contribute. Mike Brown was a practical chaplain. He accepted bad money but used it for good purposes."

"And our smuggler got to know him pretty well?"

"Yes. He says Reverend Brown *did* marry Mayura's mother, and they were very happy together. Everything happened just as Rebecca told you."

"I never doubted that Rebecca believed it. But why is Madame Piathip so determined to hide it?"

"There's a possibility that Rebecca's father invested his own savings in his wife's family business. Vatan Silk. It was just a small family operation then. Mike Brown put money into it. He bought stock, in other words."

Kash was stunned. "How much?"

"Fifty-one percent. Mike Brown owned a controlling share in Vatan Silk, according to the glimmer of information Traynor got. If it's true, Rebecca has inherited a silk company."

"Good God."

"You can't discuss any of this. It hasn't been confirmed. Don't tell her, because it would only hurt her if it can't be proved."

"For now, I've got to get her out of jail."

"Son, don't lose your objectivity—"

"I've already lost it. I've lost everything. I can't promise you I'll be objective, but I'll do what's right. Take care. I'll call you when I can. Don't worry if you don't hear from me."

"Kash! Dammit! I'm sending Traynor! Wait!"

"No time to wait. Good-bye." Kash cut the connection and dialed a new number. He had dangerous plans to make. He wasn't waiting for help, advice, or the law to set Rebecca free.

"You come now. Hurry," the guard said in a low, strident voice. "If you want to leave, you come."

Rebecca froze, a grubby towel hanging from one hand, a tepid pail of wash water by her feet. She looked around the courtyard furtively, disbelieving. The noonday sun beat down with white heat, leaving sharp shadows in the corner of the high stone walls. She stood in one of the shadows. Several dozen women milled around near the walls, trying to wash themselves and keep out of the sun.

"Escape?" Rebecca asked numbly. "Isn't that illegal?"

"Now," the guard repeated, jerking her head toward a narrow steel door in one corner.

Rebecca glanced over at Rungsima, who stood with head down, washing her arms. One look at Rungsima's strained face told her the girl was listening. "Go," Rungsima whispered, stepping closer to her. "What are you waiting for? Your man has come to get you. You are lucky. I wish I were so lucky."

Rebecca grabbed her hand. "You come too."

The guard, a wiry woman with sharp eyes, nearly yelped in surprise. "You think you make the rules? Are you crazy?"

"Are you crazy?" Rungsima echoed. "What do you care about me for?"

Because I can help you the way I wish I could have helped Kash when he was a child. Rebecca shook her head at the guard. "She's my friend. I'm not going without her. If you take us both, there'll be twice as much money for you. I guarantee it."

The guard said something dire in Thai, but her eyes flashed at the mention of money. "Hurry, *both* of you."

She led them into a maze of dirty hallways with ceilings so low that Rebecca, who was much taller than the other women, had to stoop painfully. The air was stagnant and suffocating, and soon a terrible stench crept into it. Rebecca covered her mouth to keep from gagging. They reached the end of the hall. High on the outer wall a narrow opening in the stone, covered in wire, provided the only ventilation and light. Below their feet, a large iron grate covered a gaping hole. Peering into it made Rebecca's skin crawl. All she could see was an occasional glimpse of swirling water as it caught a trace of sunlight. The water gurgled thickly, and dank air rose from it.

Rungsima moaned. "We have to go down there?"

"After dark," the guard replied. "Your friend will come for you through the sewer. You must wait here until then. Don't make a sound. Don't talk. Sit down by the grate and don't move." She started away but halted long enough to look back at Rebecca. "I'll send someone to your man for the money you promised. If I don't get it, you'll wish you were dead. Both of you."

After she left, Rebecca motioned to a spot beside the frightening sewer hole. She and Rungsima sat down against a slimy wall. The heat made it difficult to breathe. "Do you think we'll survive until nighttime?" Rungsima whispered in Rebecca's good ear.

"Yes. I'm not going to die a prisoner. And neither are you."

They put their heads on their drawn-up knees. Time crept back with maddening slowness, and there were times when claustrophobia rose in Rebecca's chest and made her heart struggle like a panicked bird. Rungsima whimpered. Finally they both curled up on their sides and pressed their faces to the cool, sticky floor.

Rebecca wasn't sure if she slept or passed out, but when she opened her eyes, the room was growing dark. She forced herself to sit up. Her head whirled. Rungsima was limp on the floor beside her. Rebecca pulled her upright and shook her lightly. Rungsima nodded and made a reassuring sound. The night air's coolness revived them a little, but the room's blackness combined with the gurgling water to produce an eerie feeling of disorientation. Rebecca's imagination began to picture every sort of creature, real and fantastic, that might slither into the pitch-dark room at any moment.

Afraid she might become hysterical, she forced herself to concentrate on images of Kash's face and body. She built a picture of him from head to foot, concentrating on details. The tiny brown mole beneath his right nipple. The sensual curves of his lips. Faint scars on his arms and legs, from boyhood escapades he wouldn't discuss, and she knew better than to ask about. She remembered the smell of his skin when he was aroused and the feel of his thighs between hers, the shifting emotions in his eyes during a conversation, the expressions that played dramatically over his handsome, intelligent face, the lilting drawl in his voice.

In the disoriented darkness he became so vivid that she suddenly realized she was crying because she loved him so much and feared she'd never see him again. Rungsima grasped her arm. "Look."

A ray of light snaked through the darkness below. They watched, hardly breathing, as it came closer. Rebecca tilted her good ear down and heard the sound of someone walking through the shallow water. Suddenly the light tilted up, blinding her and Rungsima. Shielding her eyes, Rebecca looked down into the weird shadows and made out Kash's face. "Becca!" he called in a throaty whisper. "Can you pull the grate aside?"

"Yes." She and Rungsima panted weakly and struggled for several minutes, but finally tugged the grate away from the hole. "Who's with you?" he asked. "I thought the guard was lying just to get more money, but I paid."

"This girl is my friend. She hasn't done anything wrong. I want to help her."

"That's good enough for me. Hurry."

"I'll send her first."

Rungsima slid into the hole, clutching its sides. Rebecca tried to help her, but they were both so drained of strength that Rungsima dropped limply. Kash caught her and handed her to someone. "Kovit is with me," he called. "Now you come. Don't be afraid. I'll catch you."

She dragged herself to the edge of the hole and swung her legs down. For one horrified second she was too afraid to push herself free, but then her tired mind remembered that Kash was below. "I trust my elephant," she mumbled weakly, and let herself fall.

He caught her, and though she couldn't see him in the darkness, she felt his welcome in the hard grip of his arms underneath her shoulders and legs, and in the kiss he placed on her forehead as he lifted her high against his chest. Rebecca said his name hoarsely and heard him make an agonized sound of relief.

Minutes later they were in a car speeding through the back streets of Bangkok. In the front seat Rungsima hunched next to Kovit's massive shoulder. Rebecca was curled up on the seat with her head cradled in Kash's hands. He bent over her, stroking her matted hair from her face and crooning so softly that no one but she could hear. She shut her eyes and listened to the wonderful deep sound.

Rungsima named a street. "Take me there. That's all I ask," she told Kovit. "I'm going to get my children and leave the city."

Rebecca pushed herself upright. Looking at Kash, she said, "Rungsima needs money to get away from her employer at one of the bars. Can you help her?"

"Of course." His voice was throaty and tender. He took a leather case from a knapsack in the floor, pulled a thick wad of bills from its bulging depths, and handed them over the seat to Rungsima. She cried out as she counted the money. "A fortune. A miracle!"

Kovit stopped the car on a narrow street lined with old houses. Rungsima turned in the seat and, crying, held out her hands. Rebecca hugged her. "Take care."

Rungsima kissed her cheek. "You will be blessed for your goodness."

As they pulled away, Rebecca felt Kash's arms go around her. Her strength gone, she slumped into them. "My remarkable lady," he murmured.

"Where are we going?" she asked.

"Someplace safe and private, where I can take care of you."

Her muscles turned to jelly, and she slid down until her head was pillowed on his thigh. He stroked her temple. Feeling queasy with relief and exhaustion, she sighed groggily as sleep closed in on her. She had to force her tongue to move. "Won't the police . . . look for us?"

"No. I bribed the right people. And who I couldn't bribe, I blackmailed or threatened."

She frowned at his ruthlessness, but only because she wondered what kind of danger he'd put himself in to rescue her. Kash played by rules he hadn't chosen willingly. Like Rungsima. And like herself, because the rules for a sheltered, small-town girl had been just as hard to break, though they were built on love.

"You broke the rules," she mumbled. Her mind was drifting peacefully, soothed by his caress, his nearness, and the comfort of his strong body.

He bent over her, and the last words she heard from him, troubled and hard, registered dimly in her mind. "I never promised you a hero," he whispered.

Rebecca made a sound of rebuke, fumbled for his hand, and brought it to her lips. He still doesn't understand, she thought sadly. Rebecca listened to the low hum of his breath as he kissed her ear. A dragon's purr lulled her to sleep.

It was the middle of the night, in a forest so deep nothing else seemed to exist except the delicate bamboo house with its thatched roof and rice-paper sliding doors. Kash held Rebecca close to his torso in the big, claw-footed bathtub, his legs drawn up so that her hips fit closely between them. Her head lay back on his shoulder. She was half-asleep, and though he'd fed her a nourishing meal of rice and fish soon after their arrival, her face still had a pinched, ashen look that stabbed him with concern.

She'd seen more ugliness in the past two days than even her vivid imagination could have conjured, he thought angrily. But now she knew, at least a little, about the reality of some people's lives, and how different they were from hers. What memories would she take away from her time with him? Loving ones, like now, but she'd never forget the others, either. It would have been easier to tell her about his childhood if she hadn't glimpsed the brutal reality of that life.

"Becca?" He brushed his lips over the side of her neck, and her soft murmur of appreciation made him put his arms around her in a fierce hug. "I'm going to wash your hair. You'll have to lean forward a little."

"Hmmm." She clasped her arms around his knees. Kash slid his hands up and down her naked back, frowning at the welts from insect bites, wishing that he could massage away all the small injuries and humiliations she'd suffered. He poured shampoo over her hair from a small ceramic bottle that sat among an array of oils, soaps, and medicines on a small table beside the tub.

As he worked his hands through the tangled strands, she raised her head and stretched her neck back. "You should open a beauty parlor, bub. Women would pay thousands for this kind of ecstasy."

Pleased to hear the humor in her voice, he lifted sudsy brunette hair from the nape of her neck and massaged the muscles there. "Good Lord, there's a beautiful babe under all the dirt. Not only is she brave, kind, and smart, she's got sexy freckles on her shoulders."

To his dismay she gave a low, racking sob. "I wasn't

brave. I was scared to death. I was ready to do whatever anyone told me to do, just to stay out of trouble. I saw a guard hit somebody. Just the idea of being hit was enough to terrify me."

"Being scared doesn't matter. It's what you do about it that makes you brave. And you did fine."

"Rungsima told me all about her work. She's never had a chance to be anything but a slave. The things that people have done to her made me sick. I felt so helpless and so angry on her behalf. No one should have to suffer as she has."

Kash leaned over her, numbly attempting to soothe her with his caresses. If a bar girl's stories could sicken Rebecca, his background would disgust her even more. "It's terrible to be at the mercy of heartless people." His voice was more raw with sorrow and memories than he'd expected.

Rebecca shivered in his embrace. "I kept thinking about Madame Piathip. I wanted to strangle her for using her power to hurt me. Put my hands around her throat and choke her. I've never felt that way about a person before."

"It's only natural."

"Not for me." Her shoulders slumped. She rested her cheek against his knee. Her eyes were shut tight, and defeat mingled with the fatigue in her face. "I can't take this emotional roller coaster anymore. I'll never convince her that I'm Mayura's half sister. The Nalinats will probably get me next. They've already kidnapped me, shot at me, had me followed—what will they do to top that? I think I've reached my limit. I'm so confused. What if I've been wrong? Maybe my father was lying about everything. Maybe he *was* involved in smuggling. Maybe there was no marriage, no baby—"

"Stop." Kash held her tightly and rocked a little, trying to soothe her. "This isn't how you really feel. Where's that undying optimism I love to make fun of?"

"I left it in jail. People really are cruel to each other.

And terrible things happen without any meaning or justice."

"That's reality. But reality is also hope, and compassion, and people like you, who help strangers like Rungsima." He was surprised to hear such optimism from his own lips. But it was true—Rebecca made him see how one kind person could undo some of the world's evil.

"I don't know," she said wearily. "Right now I'm afraid to learn anything else about reality." Her voice broke. "If my father was lying, I don't know how I'd stand it."

"I don't think he was. I believe him." Kash recalled the information Audubon had given him about Rebecca's father. It might not be true, but if it was, the most stunning rumor of all was that Reverend Brown had inherited a few thousand dollars and invested it in Vatan Silk at a time when the company was no more than a small family business; that Reverend Brown's modest investment had bought him a majority share of the stock.

He couldn't tell Rebecca that story until he'd confirmed it. If it was true, she'd inherited a lot of money, maybe millions. Madame Piathip had deceived her for the most selfish reasons.

"I wish I knew the truth," Rebecca said brokenly. Kash stroked her arms, then ran his hands over her breasts and stomach, not in a sexual way, but in a desperate attempt to convey his sympathy. "I believe your father was as decent and honest as you've said. That he loved Mayura's mother, married her, and lost Mayura to the Vatan family against his wishes."

"But there's no proof."

"You didn't need proof before. You had faith."

She shoved her hands into her soapy hair and bowed her head in despair. "I know, I know. I still want to believe in him. But why are the Vatans so against me? Why would Madame Piathip hide the truth after all these years? I can't hurt her, or Mayura. I don't have any power."

Kash tried to calm her by pulling her hands down and cupping them in his own. *You don't have any power unless you're the heiress of Vatan company stock*, he told her silently. All serenity gone, he warred with his secretive nature.

If he told her, he'd ease her pain and confusion temporarily. But what if the story turned out to be spurious? What Rebecca didn't know couldn't hurt her. Unproven truths were worse than none at all. She needed cheering up, but he wouldn't take the risk of giving her false hope. She'd been through too much disappointment already.

She wanted proof, not hearsay. Maybe in the bright, simple world she came from, rumors would be enough, but from Kash's point of view only absolutes counted. He made a hard decision not to tell her anything he'd discussed with his father. For now he'd do his best to distract her. He'd remind her that together, at least for tonight, they could create a beautiful world of their own.

"Becca, listen to me," he ordered gently. He let go of her hands and leaned back so he could rub her shoulders. "You can't judge your feelings right now. You need rest. You need to stop thinking about everything that's happened. Tomorrow you can worry about the future. But not tonight."

"I can't stop thinking."

"I'll help. I went through hell to rescue you. Don't I deserve some attention? Concentrate on pleasing me." He made his voice sound solemn and quaint. "You barbarian women don't know how to take care of a man."

She twisted to look at him. Tears and flecks of shampoo suds clung to her cheeks. The blue of her eyes was dull from crying. But her expression became thoughtful, and one corner of her mouth curved down in droll consideration as she studied his patient attitude. "If you weren't so smug about it, I'd tell you how much what you did meant to me."

"I knew you'd get around to showing your gratitude as soon as your mind cleared."

"You're right." She rubbed the heel of one hand over her teary cheeks in a gesture that was unconsciously childlike and vulnerable. It tugged at his heart. Her strength and determination had never revealed their tender underside so poignantly, and in that guileless moment he realized one reason he'd fallen in love with her so quickly and deeply. Whatever was left of his innocence had reached out to her with a survival instinct stronger than he'd ever believed possible.

She swiveled around with her knees drawn up tight so she could face him. Slipping her arms around his neck, she studied his face as if seeing him for the first time. The devotion in her eyes was a magnet. It drew him with unwavering power. No one had ever looked at him with such hope before.

"What you did made me love you more than ever," she said softly. "When I was in jail, my worst fear was that you'd get yourself hurt trying to help me. I'd rather have something terrible happen to me than to you."

Shaken, he struggled with a fierce need to say that he loved her, too, but lifelong habits died hard. He had always hoarded his emotions and rationed them out as small, casual gifts. She asked for his whole heart, and she offered hers, but she didn't really know him. For the first time he put a name on the bleak feeling inside his chest. Fear. Pure, deeply ingrained fear. He was horrified by the fear that someday she'd regret loving him.

"I told you I wouldn't leave you," he answered. "I meant it. You needed me, and I was there for you."

Disappointment darkened her eyes at his unsentimental reply. Her crestfallen look stabbed him. Kash fought for better words. "I couldn't eat. I couldn't sleep. I kept picturing you in a dirty jail cell, scared, confused, and being mistreated. I thought I'd go crazy if I didn't get you out."

She murmured his name and put her arms around him. "The important thing is that we're together again." Then she kissed him tenderly, letting her mouth linger on his and giving a tiny moan when he caressed her breasts. Loving her brought an overpowering hunger for her touch and an even more powerful need to please her.

He rinsed the fragrant shampoo out of her hair and smoothed his thumbs over her features with exquisite care. She tilted her face up for the gentle exploration. Her parted lips stole his attention, and he sank his mouth onto hers, teasing her with deep, thrusting motions of his tongue.

She drew her fingers down his body as if she'd never get enough of him. Her greedy caresses were delicate but confident; her wildness excited him even more. Her hands slid into the water and played over his thighs and belly, unhurried, tantalizing, bawdy. Kash inhaled sharply with pleasure.

He paid her back with the same uninhibited stroking. Her passion made her writhe and stretch out until she lay on her stomach with her body atop his. Kash sank deeper into the water. It lapped at their shoulders. His body rose to meet her soft belly as she rubbed against him.

She nuzzled her face into the crook of his neck, kissing him, then nipping his skin gently. When he arched under her, she smiled against his throat and pressed kisses upward until she reached his mouth. As he shifted with pleasure, she slid her hands between their bodies, then urged him into a quiet frenzy with her intimate cuddling.

Kash heard himself make a gruff sound of surrender. He brought one hand to the back of her head and held her hair tightly while he ground his mouth on hers. She opened to him hungrily. His savage response took the mood to a different level, one of primitive seduction.

Beneath the surface of the warm, sudsy water he grasped her bottom and delved into her with his fingers. She called his name and raised her lips to his forehead, then trailed small kisses over his eyes and cheeks. Kash lost himself in the desire blazing from her half-shut eyes. She smiled with provocative intent, but her eyes remained serious. "Catch me, if you want me."

She pushed herself upright and stood, then stepped quickly out of the tub and picked up a white towel from a wooden rack nearby. The bath area was separated from the sleeping room by a folding rice-paper screen. Drying herself slowly, her eyes never leaving his, she walked away. "You've taught me well," she called over her shoulder as she disappeared around the screen. "I know when to take charge."

Kash was too aroused to smile at her tactics. He climbed from the tub and followed her, dripping water and suds on the woven rugs, his body tight with need, his mood turbulent.

She waited beside the bed. It was only a mattress covered in white sheets atop a low platform. The stark simplicity suited the emotions churning between them. Rubbing her breasts with the thick towel, she quietly watched him approach, but he saw the swift rise and fall of her chest and the pink flush of excitement on her face. Her eyes flashed with challenge. "See? You followed me."

"Don't ever walk away from me again," he told her, snatching the towel out of her hands.

"If you don't like it, then don't ever let me leave."

"If you want to play games, then let's play mine." He grasped her wrist and pulled her swiftly to the mattress. Pinning her with his body, he latched his hands around hers and pushed them above her head. Her breath fanned his face as he bent his head to kiss her. She raised her mouth to his and nearly destroyed him with her welcome.

Within seconds they were locked together in sensual struggle, pushing at each other, stroking roughly, biting, kissing, holding each other down, using the bed as a stage where all the love, fear, and conflict between them could be acted out with mutual intensity. She gripped his jaw, tears glittering in her eyes. "Stop hiding from me."

Breathing hard, Kash cupped her face between his hands and looked down at her. Sorrow and frustration mingled with love. "Give me time," he said hoarsely. "Since I met you, I don't know who I am. I'm trying not to hurt you while I find out."

Her defenses shattered, and she took him in a tight embrace. "I love you. I'll keep saying it. You don't have to say it back. Just keep listening."

"*Becca.* I'm listening, I promise. You're killing me."

"No, I'm killing that part of you that keeps me at arm's length."

He laughed sharply. "You're not that far away, not ever. Especially not right now."

She stroked his shoulders and slowly curled her legs around him. In a barely audible voice she said, "Closer. I need you closer."

He curved his body into hers, and they held each other in hot, gentle union, moving with a rhythm that became more and more frantic until her cries exploded against his mouth. He rocked with her in wild release, dragging his lips across hers, chanting her name in a frenzy of emotion.

They collapsed silently, caressing each other, their heads burrowed together. "Are you okay?" she whispered, sounding exhausted. She kissed him and studied his face worriedly.

"No. Yes. I don't know. How about you?"

"I've been kidnapped, drugged, shot at, and thrown in jail. I'm in love with a wonderful man who's driving me out of my mind. And I don't have the vaguest idea of what's going to happen next." She tilted her forehead against his and sighed. "But I don't have any regrets."

Kash shut his eyes. He knew the future better than she did, and he feared it.

Ten

She knelt in the yard around the cottage, shaded by a palm tree in the hot midmorning sun, wearing only Kash's shirt. Quiet and troubled, she drew in a patch of smooth dirt with a sharp twig. As usual, the dragon took form easily, but capturing his spirit had become more difficult. He no longer looked evil. Instead he was puzzled and sad.

"He looks as if he's meditating," Kash said behind her. "Or having a painful attack of indigestion."

She swiveled on her heels and gazed up at him. He'd wrapped the bedsheet around his waist. It trailed to the ground and bared the muscular leg he angled to one side. Warm sunlight glowed on the golden skin of his torso and arms. His thick black hair shagged over his forehead in a way that mesmerized her because its boyish look made a stark contrast to his sensually sculpted, intense face. His eyes moved slowly from the drawing to her with a mixture of bewilderment and affection that made her melt inside.

He was the reason her body felt tender and her emotions were drained. She gave him a pensive smile. "The dragon's thinking. He can't decide how to get out of the fix he's in."

"What's that?" Kash sat down gracefully and slipped his arms around her. She leaned against him and stroked his hair back from his forehead. It was a loving gesture. "He's stuck in the middle of a tropical forest with a woman he can't help anymore."

He frowned. "What do you mean?"

"Madame Piathip has made it clear that she's through with me. I'll never get to see Mayura." Rebecca hesitated. "Unless you take me to see her."

He didn't answer. They looked directly into each other's eyes. She searched his for the reason behind his silence. "She was in Switzerland under the protection of people who work for me. But when I broke my contract with Madame Piathip, I broke my obligation to protect Mayura from the Nalinats."

"What did they threaten to do, exactly?"

"They said they'd kidnap her and force her to marry their son. To save face. It was a perfectly honorable plan, in their minds."

"You won't throw Mayura to the Nalinats, no matter how angry you are at Madame."

His eyes glowed with quiet gratitude. "You doubt my cold-blooded instincts?"

"Yep."

"All right, you know me too well. I haven't told my people to desert her." He lifted his head and glanced toward the narrow dirt road disappearing into the forest.

Rebecca tapped his chest impatiently. "Will you take me to her?"

"I don't have to. Listen. Good Lord, Traynor has the most incredible timing. We'd better go put some clothes on." Bewildered, Rebecca turned her good ear toward the road and strained to hear. She caught the sound of a vehicle approaching. Her lips parted in an *Oh!* of understanding. She whirled back to Kash. He nodded. "I've brought Mayura to you."

• • •

They sat at opposite ends of a long bamboo bench in the cottage's main room, looking at each other awkwardly. Rebecca had barely had time to rush indoors and change clothes. She'd put on a pale pink shirtwaist dress and scandals, then brushed her hair into a semblance of neatness. She knew her appearance was disheveled and unsophisticated.

But then, to her delight, so was her sister's.

Mayura Vatan was almost as tall as Rebecca, just as slender, and the ends of her short brown-black hair curved in different directions. She wore a baggy cotton top and a loose print skirt that hung unevenly around her calves. Her tilted eyes in a pretty face were framed by wide wire-rimmed glasses. She was curious, intelligent, and clumsy. The sense of kinship and recognition was so powerful that Rebecca was speechless.

"You may be my relative?" Mayura asked in beautifully accented English.

"Yes."

"Mr. Santelli has told me what my aunt did to you. You must forgive her, if you can. She's an eccentric person but a very loving one, in her own way. Her husband left her when she was young, because she couldn't have children. So I am like a daughter to her, you see. And she's very overprotective."

"I understand. I had an overprotective father."

They shared a look of growing fascination. "My aunt has always expected me to take control of Vatan Silk someday," Mayura continued. "But I'd rather be an artist. A painter." She sighed. "It's difficult to break free of tradition. I must honor my aunt's wishes."

"I'm an artist too," Rebecca said in amazement. "Well, sort of. A cartoonist."

"I know. Mr. Santelli told me all about you. I'm so impressed! But why is someone so beautiful and talented still unmarried?"

"Good taste. High expectations. And very few offers, frankly. I'm a loner."

Mayura was nodding fervently. "Yes, yes! I understand! Me too!"

Thinking pensively about Kash, Rebecca glanced toward an open window. He had changed into trousers and a thin white shirt, and outside, he was embroiled in deep conversation with the man who'd escorted Mayura from Switzerland. Traynor was a giant, redheaded, ruggedly handsome man whose permanent expression seemed to be a mysterious scowl.

"I wish I had proof that you and I are related," Rebecca told Mayura wistfully. "And I wish your aunt would explain why she wants it kept secret."

Mayura drew herself up proudly. "I want all of this explained, yes. I want the feud with the Nalinats ended too." She flashed Rebecca a grin. "So I've invited my aunt and the Nalinats here for a meeting."

Rebecca gestured numbly toward the window, where Kash and Traynor were studying a piece of paper. "Do they know?"

"No. I'm being independent. Next to rejecting Somsak Nalinat's marriage proposal, this is the most adventurous thing I've ever done. What do you think of me?"

Rebecca was worried, but she couldn't help laughing. "We *must* be related."

Rebecca's first impression of the three Nalinats was that they were undeniably handsome people, with their smooth, delicate features and regal bearing. There was Wasun, the father and head of internationally known Nalinat Silks, Sujima, the socially powerful mother, a cousin of the Thai royal family, and Somsak, the son, an unusually tall man with flashing black eyes and an arrogant smile.

They sat on plush cushions around a low ebony table, facing her and Kash. Madame Piathip sat in queenly splendor at the head of the oval table. She was the only one not dressed in Western clothes. A gold-and-pink silk sarong exposed one of her strong shoulders. Small porcelain teacups sent steamy, strong vapor into the air. Madame tapped her fingernails on her cup, for attention. Mayura sat at the other end, proudly ignoring Somsak's heated glares.

"My guest, Miss Brown, has not had a pleasant visit in our country," she told the Nalinats. Her voice was polite, but her face was a mask. "Someone has done terrible things to frighten her, as I'm sure you've heard."

"We've heard," Wasun Nalinat said stiffly. "It's shocking. Who would do such a thing to an innocent foreigner?"

Rebecca bit her tongue to keep quiet. *You would, you cold-blooded lizard.* "I could take a guess," she said politely.

Kash rubbed his knee against hers under the table, signaling her to hold her anger. He'd warned her to say as little as possible. In the hierarchy of social customs, a foreigner should be seen and not heard.

Somsak had been examining her openly ever since she and Kash had walked into the room. Now he leaned toward her across the small table and said, "I'm convinced. You are Mayura's half sister."

She blinked in surprise. "Yes."

"*No,*" Madame Piathip retorted. She looked furious. "She is mistaken. I now believe she's made an *innocent* mistake. She can't help that her father lied to her. So many foreigners would like to claim a connection to a fine family such as mine. But she is *not* my niece's relative."

"I don't agree," Wasun Nalinat said. "Look at her. There's a resemblance."

"Yes, there is," Mayura interjected eagerly.

"We're sisters," Rebecca blurted. "My father wouldn't lie."

"Silence!" Madame Piathip ordered. Kash took Rebecca's arm in a meaningful grip. *Patience,* it urged. "Excuse me," he said to the Nalinats in a gracious tone, "but perhaps the only important question is, Why do you care whether this American is or isn't related to Mayura?"

"Mayura's relatives owe us a debt of honor, just as she does," Sujima Nalinat said with great dignity. "Mayura agreed to marry my son. Everyone knew it. The merger of the Nalinat family's silk company and the Vatan Silk Company was a matter of great discussion in all the important homes of our country. Now we are shamed. Our family company is shamed. We demand that the Vatans honor the engagement of Mayura and our son, and therefore the merger of our businesses."

Rebecca's head whirled with the information. So there was more than family honor at stake. There was money and power too.

She glanced at Kash. He'd been listening with a pleasant, solemn expression on his face. Now he nodded as if in agreement but said, "The Vatan family has instructed me—as I've told your representatives before—that there was never any formal engagement between Mayura and Somsak, only friendship. This is a regrettable misunderstanding, but no breach of honor."

"There was an engagement," Somsak protested. "And there will be a marriage!" He pointed to Rebecca. "If not to Mayura, then to this one."

Madame Piathip gave a loud gasp. "I don't care if you marry this foreigner, but you'll never claim Vatan lineage through her!"

Rebecca stared at the Nalinat family speechlessly. She was dimly aware of Kash's hand tightening like a vise on her forearm. Switching her stunned gaze to him, she watched his expression harden into fearsome anger. A muscle popped in his jaw. She knew he was struggling with his emotions, and she fought an urge to grasp his hand in warning. Suddenly the smooth, cool man had become the dragon, ready to attack.

"She's not available," he said in a lethal tone. "And even if she were, an arranged marriage is out of the question."

"A half sister to the Vatan family is better than no Vatan at all," Wasun Nalinat told them. "But we have proof that this woman is related to Mayura. We have her lotus necklace."

Rebecca gasped. "The one you stole from me in a brothel!"

"It belonged to Mayura's mother. We have a photograph of her wearing the necklace." He stared hard at Madame Piathip, who suddenly looked worried. "We also suspect why Rebecca Brown is important to Vatan Silk."

Rebecca felt as if she were spinning off into space. She clasped her forehead and looked at Kash again. He met her gaze with eyes shadowed in urgency and regret. *Regret.* He knew something that he hadn't told her. She recoiled as if he'd threatened her. His lips parted in dismay, and he started to speak, but she shook her head bitterly and looked at Madame. The matriarch's half-shut eyes and guarded expression spoke volumes.

The truth hit Rebecca like a slap. "You and Kash have been hiding something from me. Both of you."

Kash twisted to face her. "I've never been Madame's confidant. What I know, I've learned on my own."

"Tell me what you know. Tell me what you were hiding," Rebecca demanded grimly.

"Not *hiding*, just holding for the right time. I wanted to confirm what I suspected. I don't deal in rumors and half-truths."

"No, you deal in secrecy," she accused in a soft, bitter tone.

Madame sputtered and slapped her teacup down. "Secrecy is a useful tool. Yes! I had my reasons for keeping family secrets! It was no concern of yours, Mr. Santelli."

"As your security coordinator, it was entirely my concern. You endangered Ms. Brown and deceived me."

"Don't question my decisions, Mr. Santelli. You did what you were hired to do—investigate a stranger who caused trouble. Why should I apologize for using my own methods, especially since they didn't work! She wouldn't leave! What an obstinate, barbaric woman!"

Mayura leaned forward eagerly. "Then you're saying she is my half sister?"

"Yes," Madame Piathip replied in a deflated voice.

"Good. I'll accept her as a wife," Somsak repeated.

Mayura made a sound of disgust. "What are you scheming about this time, Somsak? What purpose would it serve for you to marry my half sister? She's not a Vatan. She owns nothing in the family company."

"Oh?" Sujima Nalinat retorted. "Ask your aunt for the truth again, Mayura."

Rebecca stared hard into Kash's troubled eyes. "*You* know too."

"I didn't want to discuss my suspicions about Madame's motives until I had proof."

"So you let me worry, and think that my father was a criminal. Did you make up that story about my father and the art thief?"

"*No*. The man told me about your father and himself. I believed him. But"—Kash turned swiftly and looked at Madame Piathip, who coughed and fanned herself delicately with one hand—"I imagine Madame set up that interview for her own purposes. It was staged."

"You've disgraced me, Aunt," Mayura interjected in despair.

"Oh, you Vatans are so deceitful," Wasun Nalinat said victoriously. "This proves it."

Madame Piathip threw up her hands. "This has nothing to do with Mayura and your son. There was no engagement. You haven't been deceived."

Numbly Rebecca sorted through the muddled details. "Why didn't you want to admit that I'm Mayura's half sister?" she asked Madame Piathip. She avoided Kash's dark scrutiny, feeling too bewildered and hurt to risk looking at him. "What makes me such a threat?"

"Let Mr. Santelli tell you. He's entirely too good at his work." Madame glared at him reproachfully.

Rebecca met Kash's eyes again. "Tell me what was so important it was worth hurting me for."

Denial and frustration darkened his expression. "I was protecting you." He gestured for Traynor, who'd been waiting in a chair near the door. Traynor took a folded, yellowed document from an inner pocket of his sports jacket and brought it to Kash. Rebecca watched in bewilderment.

Kash, his face rigid, opened the document and placed it on the table in front of her. She read it with disbelieving eyes. It was a signed agreement spelling out her father's investment of ten thousand dollars in the Vatan Silk Company.

Kash said brusquely. "Thirty years ago, when he was stationed in Thailand with the army, your father invested his life savings in the silk company his wife's family had started. The family had almost no money and only a handful of employees."

Rebecca looked up at him. She raised a hand to her throat. "My father bought stock in the company?"

"Yes." Kash's troubled eyes were riveted to hers. "Fifty-one percent."

Her breath stalled in her lungs. "The controlling interest?"

"Yes."

"But he didn't have any stock certificates. And he never mentioned them."

Madame Piathip exhaled wearily. "He was a very obstinate and proud man."

"You mean he wouldn't take bribes from the family who'd stolen his daughter."

"Ungracious foreigner! Don't speak to me that way!"

Mayura was staring at them all in shock. "You mean

I'm not the heir of Vatan Silk? I'm free to do what I want?"

"You are heir to almost half the company's stock," Madame told her proudly. "And your father's other child, his *barbarian* child, will never take what's yours. I swear it."

"I don't want my share of the stock," Rebecca said, and shoved the document away. She felt bone-weary and defeated, even though she'd won everything and more. Kash had let her worry and grieve over her father's story, when the truth—even a tentative truth—would have meant the world to her. His secrecy wounded her more than ever, because this time it hurt not only him, but her. She'd thought him incapable of hurting her. "I'll give my stock to Mayura. All I want is to be accepted by her."

"Oh, no, you must not do this to me!" Mayura cried. She reached over and grasped Rebecca's hands. "I don't want to be in charge. I only enjoy designing the artwork on the silks. I'm an artist, not a businesswoman. Please, please, don't give the stock to me!"

"I think you should give it to us," Somsak said pompously. "We'll take it in payment for a broken engagement."

Kash bent his head close to Rebecca's ear. "Keep it," he ordered. "It's a small fortune. You can travel, meet exciting people, do whatever makes you happy—"

"I tried that already," she told him in a low, icy voice. Her body was stiff with rejection. "It wasn't all I'd hoped it would be. Someone took advantage of my faith in him. I'm ready to go back to Iowa and forget everything that happened here. Except for meeting Mayura."

Choking back tears, she looked at Mayura. "Why don't you come to Iowa and stay with me for a few weeks? I'll show you our father's mementoes, and you can meet his friends. You and I can get to know each other."

Mayura's eyes lit up. Madame slapped a hand on the table. "I forbid it."

Mayura looked at her with ruffled dignity. "I honor you, and I love you, but now it's time for me to undo the damage you've done. I want to know my other family. I want to see the world for myself. I'm going."

Madame Piathip looked chastised as never before. "I will take this under consideration."

"Thank you. I would appreciate your best wishes."

"What about our honor?" Wasun Nalinat said hotly. "We have no wedding and no business merger."

Rebecca shook her head. "You have a partnership with Vatan Silk. I swear it. No merger, but an alliance. I'm sure Madame Piathip will do business with you. I'll give her the controlling share of stock, if she'll agree to that."

Madame looked stunned. "Why? Why would you do that for me?"

"Because I want to settle the feud. Because you're part of my family, and I take that bond seriously, even if you don't."

Madame's eyes filled with tears. She bowed her head over a respectful *wai*. "I will never call you a barbarian again."

"It is done," Wasun Nalinat announced. "The feud is ended."

"And I'll go to America to visit with my sister," Mayura said happily.

Kash stood up. "I'd like to talk to Rebecca in private, please. Excuse us."

Rebecca nodded to the group and left the cottage at Kash's side. They walked beyond a curve in the forest for privacy, not speaking a word during the tense journey. He stopped her with a firm hand on her arm. "I was only waiting until I had proof, before I told you everything I knew about your father and Vatan Silk. The stock agreement was that proof. Traynor brought it to me when he brought Mayura."

"You knew about the partnership," she accused softly.

"You *knew* my father was no art smuggler and that I'm Mayura's blood relative. But you kept it secret."

"To protect you, dammit. I didn't know enough to be certain. How many times do I have to say that? I didn't want to see you get hurt or disappointed. How could I tell you that you might have inherited a fortune, and then find it out it wasn't true?"

"You didn't know me well enough to realize that my father's honor meant more to me than a stock investment?"

"Your father's story was intimately tied up with that investment."

"That's not a good reason." Her throat was on fire with restraint, and her voice shook. "Not what I've come to expect from you."

"I trust my instincts. I thought I knew what was best for you. I still think I did the right thing."

"You always believe in your secrets. I don't want to be protected like that. I want you to trust *my* instincts. But you won't. That's what hurts. Until you decide to trust me, really trust me, I'll always feel like a stranger in your life."

"You don't know what you're talking about, because you don't understand what or who I am. It's wise to remember that I'm no choirboy."

"I don't want your brand of wisdom, then."

She pulled away from him, her chest aching with emotion. This was the hardest moment of her life, the hardest words she'd ever had to say. "You can't believe how much I love you. If you had faith in me, you'd know. If you can ever bring yourself to say what needs to be said, you know where to find me. I'm going to leave you." Tears streamed down her face.

His expression was tortured as he stared at her. "I know what's best. I'm trying to save us both some pain." He held out his hands to her. "I can't share everything you want. But I don't want to lose you."

"You said that you'd never leave me, that I'd leave you.

Dear Lord, I didn't believe you. But you were right. You're making me leave. You've never told me that you love me. You can't even say it now, can you?"

"Would it make you stay? Is that all it would take? To hear something you already know is true?"

She pressed her hands to her mouth to keep from crying out loud. After struggling a moment, she managed to whisper, "You won't admit it, because you don't want to make any promises to me."

"How can I?" he said in a raw voice. "Go home to Iowa. Remind yourself of your real life, the people you admire, the kind of world they share with you. Those are the promises you need."

She hugged herself to keep from breaking apart. "I need you, but not your secrets." He made a move to take her in his arms, but she backed away. "Can Traynor take Mayura and me to Bangkok? I want to leave."

His arms dropped to his sides, and his face tightened. "He can take you right away. Good. That's the best thing to do." Devastated, she gave him a look that made him wince. "I hurt too," he whispered, touching the center of his chest. "My whole life is wound up inside me like a chain. You don't know how hard it is to break that hold."

Rebecca laid a hand over his. "I thought I could break it for you. But I can't. I'll never be able to."

She walked away. But she knew the bond between them was also a chain. It would reach all the way home, and hold her for the rest of her life.

Eleven

Clouds came up and the wind rose. The air carried the scent of rain, and scattered drops flung themselves past her windows. Rebecca felt as bleak as the spring afternoon. The temperature dropped, and she shivered. Without Mayura to help her keep her spirits up, she wandered around the house, ignoring the work waiting on the drawing board in her studio, restless, aching with loneliness.

After four weeks of having Mayura there day and night, always talking and laughing, it was time to face reality. Mayura had gone home to Thailand. There'd been no word from Kash since the day at the cottage. Audubon had called twice to ask how she was doing, the first time saying that Kash was working out of the country, somewhere in Europe, on a new assignment.

Rebecca slumped down in a comfortable old sofa chair by her living-room window and watched the wind whip the new green leaves of the oaks in her front yard. There were no cars on the quiet residential street, a place as pretty as a postcard, with neat little houses built not long after World War II. As with her home, each had flowers and large shade trees in the yards.

She aimlessly creased a fold in the skirt of her print

sundress. Audubon's second phone call had come yesterday. She'd just returned from taking Mayura to the airport. She and her sister had made plans to spend time together again, within a few months. Audubon had been pleased to hear it.

"You went to a lot of trouble to find her, but it seems worth it," he said.

"A million times," she agreed.

"Even considering the problem between you and my son?"

"I'll never regret knowing Kash. Well, *trying* to know him." She had struggled with a catch in her throat, though she doubted Audubon was fooled by her casual tone. "Did Kash ask you to call?"

"Not in so many words. He'll either call you himself or not at all. He believes in suffering alone with his misery. But when I told him I'd called you the first time, he asked me a hundred questions about everything you'd said."

"And?"

"He thinks he did the right thing by letting you go. I'm calling to tell you that he finished his work in Europe yesterday."

Her heart pounded. "Do you think he'll come here?"

"I don't know. What will you say if he does?"

"That nothing has changed. That missing him is the worst pain I've ever felt."

"Why don't you get on a plane and come to Virginia?"

"And confront him in his own home? I couldn't. He's too private. He'd only resent me."

"You seem to think he's made of stone. He's not. No one has ever turned him inside out the way you have."

"It's mutual."

"Come to Virginia. Stay with my wife and me. Our estate makes good neutral territory for a meeting with Kash."

"I can't. Not because of pride—I'd do anything if I thought he'd open up to me. But I won't track him down just to hear him say that we don't belong together." She was crying now. "I'll always love him, and I'm not giving up. But the decision has to be his."

Audubon had sighed and said something about watching Kash waste years on regrets. He had promised to keep in touch with her.

Rebecca's mind wandered dully from that conversation to the windswept spring day again. She felt like a trapped animal in a neat, clean, respectable cage. Hugging herself, she went to the kitchen to make a cup of coffee, but decided it had no appeal. She tried to read a book, but her thoughts kept going to Kash. Every fiber of her body and mind called out to him. Finally she climbed into bed, fully clothed, and curled up facing an open window, staring into the rain, which now came down in a steady trickle. The air smelled like loneliness to her.

Lost in despair, she didn't hear a car pull up by her front walk or the footsteps on her porch. The sudden sound of heavy knocking on her front door made her jump.

When she went into the living room, she looked through the door's glass panes and halted, stunned. Kash.

She flung the door open and stared up at him. The wind billowed his long black raincoat and tousled his hair. The open coat revealed a sleek black pullover and black trousers. He even wore black shoes. His face was lean, sharp, and grim. His eyes were riveted to her from the moment she opened the door. They glittered with unhappiness.

"I waited until Mayura left," he said brusquely. "Then I had to come to see you and tie up the loose ends."

Rebecca realized that her hands had risen to her throat in shock. She was speechless, and when she finally found her voice, it was hoarse with disbelief. "You've been watching me?"

"Yes, my secretive black soul had someone keep track

of Mayura's visit. I didn't want to interfere with your time together. But now she's gone, and I want to finish what you started in Thailand."

"Finish it? In what way?"

He gave a curt nod toward her comfortable pastel furnishings, and cozy fireplace. "Good God, it's just the way I pictured it."

"Did you come here to do a decorator's review of my house?"

"No, to see you in your natural habitat. *Cartoona Iowana* in her nest."

"So you want to convince yourself that I'm as corny as you expected?"

"That's right. Since you walked out on me as if I were to blame, I want to show you how right I was to let you leave. I'm going to get this over with so we can move on with our lives."

"Our separate lives, you mean. Our lonely, miserable, unfulfilled lives."

"*Different,*" he emphasized between clenched teeth. "Different lives."

"Only because you insist that you're not fit company for me."

"Not fit company? What the hell?"

"Obviously you think you're not good enough for me. Why else would you keep trying to chase me off?" She held out her hands. "What man would turn down all my crazy adoration?"

"Stop giving me that baby-blue stare of challenge. Let me in."

"Sure. Come in and make yourself at home." She mockingly swept her arm in a grand gesture of invitation. He stepped in, shrugged his raincoat off, but held it clenched in one hand. Rebecca shook her head. "I have old-fashioned notions, of course, but I think it's rude of you to drip on my braided rugs. You'll have to give me the coat. Don't worry, I won't spray cinnamon perfume on it or pin a sprig of flowers to the lapel. You'll leave with your sophistication untouched."

He frowned and handed her the coat. Their fingers met as she took it, and the tension reached an explosive peak. They froze, looking at each other desperately, with the pretense stripped away for a second. She ached to put her arms around him. She could actually feel herself being pulled toward him.

Rebecca almost jerked the coat from his grip. Breathing roughly, she made herself concentrate on shaking the raincoat out and carrying it to a row of brass hooks on the foyer wall. She tossed it on one haphazardly. "Ready for your getaway."

She clasped her trembling hands behind her back and pivoted to face him. "My house is messy. I'm not an organized person. But I'm clean, and I can make a decent cup of coffee. In other words, follow me to the kitchen."

The whole time, he hadn't budged. His gaze had never left her, and the combination of anger and tenderness in it made her knees weak. "If you came to make fun of me, you're losing points," Rebecca told him. "Say something."

His concentration broke, and he looked at her wearily. "I don't want any coffee." He walked into the living room and stopped in the center. Rebecca followed him numbly. He was a powerful, dark figure who charged the tame atmosphere with energy. "You're absorbing all the light," she joked. "I'll have to turn on the lamps if you don't stop."

"Did you paint the watercolor landscapes?" he asked, staring at a wall filled with framed canvases. He made it sound like an accusation.

"Yep. I confess."

"They're so different from your cartoons. They flow. There aren't any definite lines."

"I see the world that way. Sort of blending together. No

way to tell where one person or place ends and another begins."

He faced her. His stance was defensive—long legs braced apart, hands clenched by his sides, head up. "But you're wrong. There are boundaries everywhere. Invisible lines that people can't cross, no matter how much they want to."

"Not in my world."

"Not in your fantasies. But I'm talking about real life. Real prejudices. Those are drawn so clearly that people can read them like a map. That's how we recognize where we belong."

"I hate maps. I'm an explorer. I want uncharted territory." She took a deep breath and added shakily, "I want you."

"What you and I want is beside the point. Because it wouldn't work."

Rebecca exploded with anger. "*Don't* say that to me again. Not ever. Make up any excuse you need for your feelings, but don't try to make me believe we're wrong for each other."

He cursed bitterly. "This is getting us nowhere." He shoved his hands in his trouser pockets and walked into her cheerful, cluttered little kitchen. Rebecca trailed him to the door and stood there, every nerve taut. He went to the dish drainer and picked up one of the odd-looking pottery mugs she collected. It had a cherubic face on the side. "I call those my muse mugs," Rebecca explained, knowing how silly it sounded. "Muse. My inspiration. Get it? You'll find all sorts of goofy things around my house."

Kash set the mug down. "You're a harmless nut."

He opened the back door and stepped out on a screened porch. Rebecca felt his torment. It bewildered her, frightened her, but finally compelled her to follow him again. They stood on the porch among white wicker chairs and a large collection of houseplants. The rain pelted the roof. The backyard was small and enclosed by a wooden fence covered in flowering vines. A big apple tree stood in the middle. Tiny green apples already filled the branches. "Look at this, the perfect setting for Miss Heartland's tea parties," Kash said dryly.

His sarcasm wounded her strained emotions. Feeling tears well up in her eyes, she pushed the porch door open and walked out into the yard. Her hands knotted by her sides, she tilted her head back and let raindrops disguise her pain. She welcomed the coldness of the water.

The porch door slammed, signaling Kash's approach. She went to the apple tree without looking back, grabbed the tip of a low branch, and doused herself with the water collected on its leaves. Kash came to her and stopped by her side. She felt his gaze on her face. Quickly she tugged at another branch, showering him with water too.

She shut her eyes and cried silently. When she looked at him again, she found stark sorrow on his face. Rain was soaking his hair and trickling down his jaw. He reached up, plucked a green apple, then held it out to her. "If this is Eden, then at the moment I feel like the snake," he said gruffly.

She shook her head. "This isn't any kind of paradise. It's just the place where I live. It doesn't define me the way you think it does. Whether I lived in a palace or a slum, I'd still be a problem for you. Because you still wouldn't have enough faith in me."

He threw the apple aside with a small, violent flick of his hand. "As I said before, I came here to tie up loose ends. To give you what you want."

She stared at him. "What I want?"

"What you *think* you want." He walked out from under the tree and stood with his head back as she had done, letting the rain fall onto his face. "The damned truth, Becca. The almighty, soul-sharing facts." His voice rose. "And then this will all be over. I won't have any secrets, and you won't hate me anymore. And it'll be a helluva lot easier for you to forget me."

She rushed over to him and grabbed the front of his black pullover. "I don't hate you, and I'll never forget you."

Looking down at her with a fierce, tormented expression, he staggered as if he'd been punched. "Do you want to know about my childhood, Becca?"

"Yes. Everything."

"Everything? You're sure?"

She took his face between her hands. The moisture running down his skin could have been raindrops or tears. "Tell me," she ordered gently.

"My mother worked in a brothel." He paused, a sick grimace on his face, his eyes watching her as if they were a condemned man's watching the executioner's switch. "And so did I."

Rebecca exhaled raggedly. "Keep talking."

"She was killed by one of her customers. An American soldier. I was five years old. Until then, she'd protected me. But after that, for the next three years, until Audubon noticed me when he came in looking for a soldier who'd gone AWOL, I was, to put it bluntly, a child whore. I didn't have a choice."

She leaned against him and rested her head on his shoulder. "I wish I could kill every person who abused you."

"That would be a long list. Mostly men." The agony in his voice raked her like a sharp blade. "Do you understand now, Becca? Don't try to tell me it doesn't matter. Deep down, it changes everything between us. Now that you know—"

"I've known for a long time." He jerked as if she'd slapped him. She lifted her head and looked up reassuringly. "Audubon told me when he came to Thailand. Don't be angry with him. I know he's never told anyone else, but he must have realized that I was different. He loves you so much, and he wanted to make certain I loved you too. He told me if I had problems with your past, to keep them to myself and let you go without hurting you. I swore that I would."

"So he told me everything about your childhood. I asked him to be explicit, because I needed to know who'd hurt you, and how, so I could try to break through to you. But I knew you'd have to tell me on your own, for it to mean anything."

Kash wiped a hand over his eyes and studied her as if a cloud had lifted from his vision. "All this time, you knew what I'd been." His voice was leaden with shock.

"Yes." Her voice soothing, she emphasized, "I knew *before* I made love to you the first time. *Before* I told you I wanted to have a life with you. I didn't fall in love with some fantasy image of you. I knew exactly what kind of man I was getting, and that made you even more precious to me."

He was no longer staring at her in blank amazement. Slowly life began returning to his eyes. "I didn't want you to pity me." He made a raw sound of distress. "And I couldn't stand the idea that anything about me might be repulsive to you. There are a lot of people who think I've been branded for life."

"Those people are fools. They don't count."

Her calm, confident tone made his expression soften. Awe and belief were replacing his fear. But his gaze remained locked on hers, studying her reaction. "Only you count," he said hoarsely.

"Then you've got nothing to worry about." Rebecca stroked his hair and kept one hand against his cheek. She caressed the taut golden skin slowly. "What happened to you didn't change the good, caring, strong spirit inside you. That spirit makes you so special. After Audubon told me about your childhood, I wanted you *more* than before."

"*Becca.*" His arms went around her in a desperate embrace. She returned it, clinging to him silently. They held each other in the rain, with their heads bent together and eyes shut. The stark power of the emotions between them made her shiver and press herself closer as his arms tightened possessively.

"I love you dearly," he whispered. "God, I've wanted to say that for so long."

She kissed him, starting a chain reaction that became a joyous, tearful reunion. They swayed together and collapsed on the wet, soft carpet of grass, touching, hugging, their legs entwined and hands moving quickly to destroy all the old loneliness.

"I have a bedroom," she announced breathlessly.

He stopped kissing her long enough to say, "Do you? How thoughtful of you."

"I knew I'd need it for something besides sleeping someday."

"I expect it's a pleasant place."

"With a queen-sized bed and beautiful Thai silk coverlets. Mayura gave them to me."

"Becca, are you trying to seduce me?"

"Are you trying to resist?"

He slid his arms under her and looked at her with devotion. "Not anymore. Not ever again."

He carried her into her bedroom and stretched out beside her on the cool, plush covers. Lifting her mouth to his, she quivered at his deep sighs. He sounded relieved and truly relaxed for the first time. They shared a look brimming with tenderness.

"Marry me," he said.

"Yes." She drew her hands around his head and cupped his face gently. "Marry *me.*"

"Yes," he answered immediately. "I'll cut back on my traveling, and when I can, I'll take you with me. And I'll always encourage your career."

"I'll move to Virginia."

"We'll build a new house, if you don't like mine."

"Someday we'll have children. And they'll love you as much as I do."

"That's more than I can imagine."

"I'll pick out a dog who doesn't snore."

A startled laugh burst from him, then another, and then she began laughing too. They held each other and rocked silently, lost in the warmth and hope of the future, giddy with emotion. He undressed her tenderly, then let her do the same for him.

They savored more kisses, and took a long time for promises, caresses, serious smiles, urgent whispers, and the slow, wild melting into each other's bodies that made them complete. The rain lulled them to sleep under the magnificent silk spreads, wrapped in each other's arms inside a cocoon of trust.

Kash woke to the soft scratching sound of her pencil moving confidently over paper. She was propped up close beside him, barely out from under the covers. He raised his head from the pillow of her breasts, kissed each of them, and looked up at her. In her hand was a small drawing pad she kept on the nightstand. "Oh, no, another dragon," he said solemnly.

Grinning, she slid down beside him and nuzzled his cheek. "See?"

This time there was a pair, looking pleasantly sly as they curled their tails around each other. Kash touched the drawing with a fingertip. "You've finally made him look happy."

"That's the she-dragon."

"Well, the other one looks happy too. How can you tell them apart?"

"That's a question only dragons can answer. It's very personal."

He tossed her pencil and pad aside, then pulled her to him. "Let's spend a few dozen lifetimes figuring it out."

She put her arms around him and smiled. "*Now*, you understand."

THE EDITOR'S CORNER

LOVESWEPT sails into autumn with six marvelous romances featuring passionate, independent, and truly remarkable heroines. And you can be sure they each find the wonderful heroes they deserve. With temperatures starting to drop and daylight hours becoming shorter, there's no better time to cuddle up with a LOVESWEPT!

Leading our lineup for October is **IN ANNIE'S EYES** by Billie Green, LOVESWEPT #504. This emotionally powerful story is an example of the author's great skill in touching our hearts. Max Decatur was her first lover and her only love, and marrying him was Anne Seaton's dream come true. But in a moment of confusion and sorrow she left him, believing she stood in the way of his promising career. Now after eleven lonely years he's back in her life, and she's ready to face his anger and furious revenge. Max waited forever to hurt her, but seeing her again ignites long-buried desire. And suddenly nothing matters but rekindling the old flame of passion. . . . An absolute winner!

Linda Cajio comes up with the most unlikely couple—and plenty of laughter—in the utterly enchanting **NIGHT MUSIC**, LOVESWEPT #505. Hilary Rayburn can't turn down Devlin Kitteridge's scheme to bring her grandfather and his matchmaking grandmother together more than sixty years after a broken engagement—even if it means carrying on a charade as lovers. Dev and Hilary have nothing in common but their plan, yet she can't catch her breath when he draws her close and kisses her into sweet oblivion. Dev wants no part of this elegant social butterfly—until he succumbs to her sizzling warmth and vulnerable softness. You'll be thoroughly entertained as these two couples find their way to happy-ever-after.

Many of you might think of that wonderful song "Some Enchanted Evening" when you read the opening scenes of **TO GIVE A HEART WINGS** by Mary Kay McComas, LOVESWEPT #506. For it is across a crowded room that Colt McKinnon first spots Hannah Alexander, and right away he knows he must claim her. When he takes her hand to dance and feels her body cleave to his with electric satisfaction, this daredevil racer finally believes in love at first sight. But when the music stops Hannah escapes before he can discover her secret pain. How is she to know that he would track her down, determined to possess her and slay her dragons? There's no resisting Colt's strong arms and tender smile, and finally Hannah discovers how wonderful it is to fly on the wings of love.

A vacation in the Caribbean turns into an exciting and passionate adventure in **DATE WITH THE DEVIL** by Olivia Rupprecht, LOVESWEPT #507. When prim and proper Diedre Forsythe is marooned on an island in the Bermuda Triangle with only martial arts master Sterling Jakes for a companion, she thinks she's in trouble. She doesn't expect the thrill of Sterling's survival training or his spellbinding seduction. Finally she throws caution to the wind and surrenders to the risky promise of his intimate caress. He's a man of secrets and shadows, but he's also her destiny, her soulmate. If they're ever rescued from their paradise, would her newfound courage be strong enough to hold him? This is a riveting story written with great sensuality.

The latest from Lori Copeland, **MELANCHOLY BABY,** LOVE-SWEPT #508, will have you sighing for its handsome hell-raiser of a hero. Bud Huntington was the best-looking boy in high school, and the wildest—but now the reckless rebel is the local doctor, and the most gorgeous man Teal Anderson has seen. She wants him as much as ever—and Bud knows it! He understands just how to tease the cool redhead, to stoke the flames of her long-suppressed desire with kisses that demand a lifetime commitment. Teal shook off the dust of her small Missouri hometown for the excitement of a big city years ago, but circumstances forced her to return, and now in Bud's arms she knows she'll never be a melancholy baby again. You'll be enthralled with the way these two confront and solve their problems.

There can't be a more appropriate title than **DANGEROUS PROPOSITION** for Judy Gill's next LOVESWEPT, #509. It's bad enough that widow Liss Tremayne has to drive through a blizzard to get to the cattle ranch she's recently inherited, but she knows when she gets there she'll be sharing the place with a man who doesn't want her around. Still, Liss will dare anything to provide a good life for her two young sons. Kirk Allbright has his own reasons for wishing Liss hasn't invaded his sanctuary: the feminine scent of her hair, the silky feel of her skin, the sensual glow in her dark eyes—all are perilous to a cowboy who finds it hard to trust anyone. But the cold ache in their hearts melts as warm winter nights begin to work their magic. . . . You'll relish every moment in this touching love story.

FANFARE presents four truly spectacular books next month! Don't miss out on **RENDEZVOUS,** the new and fabulous historical novel by bestselling author Amanda Quick: **MIRACLE**, an unforgettable contemporary story of love and the collision of two worlds, from critically acclaimed Deborah Smith: **CIRCLE OF PEARLS**, a thrilling historical by immensely talented Rosalind Laker; and **FOREVER**, by Theresa Weir, a heart-grabbing contemporary romance.

Happy reading!

With warmest wishes,

Nita Taublib

Nita Taublib
Associate Publisher/LOVESWEPT
Publishing Associate/FANFARE

FANFARE SPECIAL OFFER

Be one of the first 100 people to collect 6 FANFARE logos (marked "special offer") and send them in with the completed coupon below. We'll send the first 50 people an autographed copy of Fayrene Preston's THE SWANSEA DESTINY, on sale in September! The second 50 people will receive an autographed copy of Deborah Smith's MIRACLE, on sale in October!

The FANFARE logos you need to collect are in the back of LOVESWEPT books #498 through #503. There is one FANFARE logo in the back of each book.

For a chance to receive an autographed copy of THE SWANSEA DESTINY or MIRACLE, fill in the coupon below (no photocopies or facsimiles allowed), cut it out and send it along with the 6 logos to:

FANFARE Special Offer
Department CK
Bantam Books
666 Fifth Avenue
New York, New York 10103

- - - - - - - - - - - - - - - - - - - -

Here's my coupon and my 6 logos! If I am one of the first 50 people whose coupon you receive, please send me an autographed copy of THE SWANSEA DESTINY. If I am one of the second 50 people whose coupon you receive, please send me an autographed copy of MIRACLE.

Name _____

Address _____

City/State/Zip _____

Offer open only to residents of the United States, Puerto Rico and Canada. Void where prohibited, taxed or restricted. Allow 6-8 weeks after receipt of coupon for delivery. Bantam Books is not responsible for lost, incomplete or misdirected coupons. If your coupon and logos are not among the first 100 received, we will not be able to send you an autographed copy of either MIRACLE or THE SWANSEA DESTINY. Offer expires September 30, 1991.

Bantam Books   SW 9 - 10/91

A man and a woman who couldn't have been more different -- all it took to bring them together was a...

Miracle
by
Deborah Smith

An unforgettable story of love and the collision of two worlds. From a shanty in the Georgia hills to a television studio in L.A., from the heat and dust of Africa to glittering Paris nights -- with warm, humorous, passionate characters, MIRACLE weaves a spell in which love may be improbable but never impossible.

ON SALE IN OCTOBER 1991

The long-awaited prequel to the "SwanSea Place" LOVESWEPT series.

The SwanSea Destiny

by Fayrene Preston

Socialite Arabella Linden was a flamboyant as she was beautiful. When she walked into the ballroom at SwanSea Place leading two snow-white peacocks, Jake Deverell knew the woman was worthy prey. . . . And at the stroke of midnight as the twenties roared into the new year 1929, Jake set out to capture the lovely Arabella, and quickly found he was no longer a man on the prowl -- but a man ensnared.

ON SALE IN SEPTEMBER 1991

THE SYMBOL OF GREAT WOMEN'S FICTION FROM BANTAM
Ask for these titles at your favorite bookstore.

AN 360 - 10/91

THE LATEST IN BOOKS
AND AUDIO CASSETTES